I0715244

EDITED BY

Paula Dias Garcia,
Sam Agar,
Marc Clohessy &
Aran Kelly

LIMERICK

2024

the garden

Sans.
PRESS

THE GARDEN

ISBN: 978 1 7391383 9 4
Published by Sans. PRESS
November 2024
Limerick, Republic of Ireland

COVER ARTWORK by Laura Callaghan
ILLUSTRATIONS by Jacob Mooij & Janus de Winter
LAYOUT & BOOK DESIGN by Paula Dias Garcia
TYPESET in Calendas Plus and Colosseum

EDITORS
Paula Dias Garcia, Sam Agar,
Marc Clohessy & Aran Kelly

www.sanspress.com
@PressSans
sans.press
/sans.press

THE GARDEN receives
financial assistance from the Arts Council.

PAULA DIAS GARCIA

EDITOR'S NOTE

The last step in each one of our collections is to look back to the start. Once all of the stories have been read, and all of the choices have been made, from selection to typesetting, we look back to our submission call to see what it was exactly we'd been looking for this time around.

And it's almost funny to see that we've described *The Garden* as stories of what happens "between bloom and decay", as if such a thing remotely resembles a straight line. As if the *circle of life* narratives we were looking for would actually be *circles*, neat and perfect and closed; no messiness, no changing of directions, no wobbling. If we were to write it now, we'd have the sense to ask for squiggles, doodles, messy sketches.

Because, both in life and in literature, we're not really believers in neat gardens. When truly vibrant and alive, gardens are messy, busy, full of bugs; they're very far removed from tidy lawns. And also, for better or worst, they will refuse to follow any sense of order. Fruit will drop from trees without ever ripening, skipping straight to rot; beautiful flowers will smell horrendous; visiting snails will decide that your beloved, prize-winning orchid is actually a pretty good snack.

What *The Garden* offers to all of us, then, is a taste of its real-life counterpart: a selection of surprises. Some of them heartbreaking, some of them life-affirming, they are what happens when wildness refuses to be contained by human boundaries. There are creatures carrying omens and regrets, relationships bursting into pulp, plants and pests demanding too much of their carers, and dark secrets refusing to remain buried, breaking through plant, ground and even skin. And always – always – *life*, demanding to be seen, to exist, to shape the world around it, against all odds, even as it ends.

In our small patch of grass, a plant is a plant, and a bird is a bird, and they're full of their own meaning and existence. But we are human, and so a plant is also the vessel for our deepest struggles, and a bird carries in its flight a lifetime of regret. In each of these stories, nature comes through in all of its gory beauty, and we're too human to avoid seeing our own selves reflected back at us.

We're so grateful to everyone that helped bring our bit of green come into bloom – the endlessly supportive writers, lectures and booksellers; the Arts Council; our featured illustrator, Laura Callaghan; and, as ever, every single one of our readers!

Welcome to the garden! We hope you're looking forward to being surprised.

THE
STORIES

CONTENT WARNINGS

Injury detail: *you've got to get them out…, Triphyophyllum sanguis*
    (of an animal): *The Rabbit, Stagnate*
    (of a child): *The Worm, Fruit of the Earth*
Death of a child: *The Rabbit, To the God of Teeth*
Childbirth: *you've got to get them out…,*
Pregnancy loss: *The Harebell*
Large scale death: *The Harebell (implied)*
Body horror: *To the God of Teeth*

IMAGE LIST

The images used in the interior composition of *The Garden* are, as follows:

Veg, by Laura Callaghan, reprinted with permission from the artist, *p. 1, 3.*
Untitled, by Sofie De Smyter, reprinted with permission from the artist, *p. 37, 39, 41, 44, 46, 48, 50, 54.*

Public domain images, obtained through the online archive of the Rijksmuseum, Amsterdam.

Donation from the heirs of Mrs. GL Arnold Bik-Stemfoort:
Konijn in hok, by Jacob Mooij, *p. 11*

A.J.J. de Winter Bequest:
Prints by Janus de Winter

Struikgewas met hagedis en nachtvlinder, *p. 10, 96, 116, 130, 148, 160, 172, 190*

Hagedis, *p. 9*

Slang met orchidee, *p. 21*

Hagedis op een boomstam, *p. 57*

Vogeltje, *p. 75*

Twee boomstammen, *p. 77*

Paddenstoelen, *p. 87*

Orchideeën, *p. 97*

Zeemonster, *p. 103*

Waterlelies, *p. 117*

Vlinder op een bloem, *p. 131*

Plant met bloem, *p. 149*

Orchidee, *p. 161*

Berglandschap, *p. 173*

Twee vogels op een tak, *p. 191*

Klaprozen met vlinder, *p. 205*

"Our grapes fresh from the vine,
Pomegranates full and fine,
Dates and sharp bullaces,
Rare pears and greengages,
Damsons and bilberries,
Taste them and try"

Goblin Market, **CHRISTINA ROSSETTI**

"It is later than you think."
[Serius est quam cogitas]

ROMAN SUNDIAL INSCRIPTION

SEAN MICHAEL

THE
RABBIT

You've been hiking for a long while. The pack has grown heavier with each bend and switchback; heavier with each tick of your wristwatch. Each tick steadily throws further and darker shadows as the sun hovers above the treeline. You must be close. *Around this next bend*, you think.

A faint buzzing enters your awareness. You don't hear it, not like the crunch of the dirt and twigs, but it's there, somewhere. It grows by fractions of degrees, imperceptible but eventually it's a ringing that pervades everything. It's like tinnitus, though you've never experienced that before; you wouldn't know what it feels like, but it's the closest thing. The wind picks up and a chill runs down your spine. The trees are rustling but there is no noise, only the pitchy ring. The branches and leaves dance in slow motion as you near the bend ahead of you.

Then you hear something over the siren. A rustling to your left as you round the bend and first catch sight of the clearing and the cabin at its centre. A flash of grey and this de-realised space that has overcome your awareness crashes inward. It isn't violent, but it is jarring as sensation returns to you, fully formed and all at once.

The rabbit stares at you from the centre of the path, before the clearing. You squint against the sun behind the cabin, behind the rabbit. Red eyes connect with yours and for a moment you see your crimson reflection before a darkening forest. Impossible from that distance, but there it is. There you are.

It's gone. A spray of dirt settles but dust motes hang in the air, and you realise you aren't squinting anymore. You look to your right and the forest is darker, the shadows merging. You resist the urge to check your watch, and you don't know why. You step forward, through the dust, towards the cabin.

Once inside, you unshoulder the pack and relief floods your sore form. It hadn't been as heavy at the beginning, but then it never is. You tend to break at the very end, not before. The weight grows with each step, but it ratchets up by degrees. Eventually it's too much to carry, but never before it can't be. You can't let it, you're responsible for too much–

You exhale a breath, a deep long-held breath, and kneel to unpack. You notice a strange, almost sterile smell and then it's gone. Sitting cross-legged on your sleeping bag, you open your laptop. As you write, the shadows of twilight darken, the glow of the laptop bleeds and dissipates, and the only other light is thrown dimly from the lantern.

You wake stiff and sore. You change and step out into the light of a new day. You can already feel your body's circadian rhythm aligning with the sun. The air is crisp; goosebumps raise on your forearms and neck. With each step through the clearing your muscles release and your tendons relax.

The river is ice as you fill the bag, your fingers numb by the time you hang it from a nearby tree to filter. You pat your hands dry on your faded jeans and once the bottles are filled the cold sting has faded. You step into the river, the water rushing around your hiking boots. You feel the water's chill, your feet dry. You stay there a while, watching the morning.

Coffee. Breakfast. Then you are at the computer, outside in the hammock, swaying with the warming breeze. The keyboard becomes rhythmic, clicking and tapping on and on as the page turns over once, twice, and again, and again. You keep writing. Sometime later you close the lid, swing out of the hammock, and walk back to the cabin. You plug the laptop into the battery pack and watch the first of four LED lights begin to blink.

Warmth arrives, the kind that only exists at midday in early October. You change into shorts and leave the cabin. You check your phone for the first time and are relieved to see that it is still searching for a signal. You search for a path lead-ing into the forest. Not the one you took here, somewhere new. You walk around the cabin and see a worn trail at the back of the clearing.

You should turn around soon. The laptop will be charged by the time you get back. You give yourself five more minutes down the trail, checking your watch for reference. Reference is everything, it's how one orients. A landmark on a drive, the time spent walking down a trail, a frantic call in the night – the one you've been waiting for and praying you never get. Without these moments of finality, we lose track of before and after. Without these things it is easy to become lost. You come around the final bend.

Lying on the forest floor is a rabbit. Your rabbit. You don't know how you know, but you can tell. Its entrails are spread, partially eaten, and you can see the light fading from those red eyes. This happened recently, minutes, moments ago. How did you not hear it? The rabbit is suffering, and you can see – almost feel – the pain. So, you draw your knife and do the only thing you can.

You return the way you came, occasionally checking your watch but otherwise keeping your eyes down. You love an-imals, but the lesser of two evils is still evil and you feel it deep, with each step away from the rabbit, from those eyes still on you.

At the river, you splash freezing water on your face, hoping it will rinse your mind as well. Looking down, you see red dripping through your fingers. You splash more water. There's more red. Heart racing, you see the red spreading through the torrent down and upstream. There, on the shore, the rabbit stares, dragging spilled and torn organs, and behind those a dark and viscous trail. You can't move, pierced by those eyes. The red torrent sweeps your feet, and you begin to fall.

You wake in your sleeping bag, sweat drenched and shivering. The cabin door is open, as is your laptop beside you. Your frantic eyes pass between the two, and you notice something you don't remember writing. Struggling with the damp polyester, you stumble to the door, then slam it. The birds from a nearby tree scatter. The light of dawn is breaking through the window. Running your hands through your hair, you realise you are still wearing your shorts from yesterday. You don't remember returning, writing more, going to bed, or leaving the door open. You shake against the discomfort of losing time.

You breathe deep and return to the sleeping bag, turn it inside out, and tuck into the now cold but dry inside. You turn to the laptop and scroll up the pages to the last thing you remember writing before the walk. You begin to read.

The sun is warming the morning air when you finish, and the low battery icon appears. You shut the lid and plug it back into the charger; the third of four LED lights begin to blink. You emerge from your sleeping bag for the second time this morning, pick up a full water bottle and walk outside. You pour the contents over your head and the chill does its job. You are now fully awake.

It's good, but you don't like it. You don't remember writing it. It's the crucial pivot from first act to second that you couldn't find. If you don't remember writing it, was it really you? If you can't remember how you got there, then how can you know where it goes?

You find yourself back at the stream with the filter bag, cautious. *But that was a dream*, you tell yourself. You've been under so much pressure, keeping it together until the end of each day is all you've been able to focus on. But the shape of your life is cracking; this garden you've tended, spiderwebs crisscrossing its surface. And you think, *here you are, out here in the woods, while they... while he–* the thought whips and leaves a stinging, bloody gash across your mind. You breathe. You remember the breathing exercises, the grounding exercises. The cabin to retreat to. You remember that the tighter you hold this broken thing you used to call your existence, the faster it shatters. The faster he's gone. *He's dying*, you think, and you step into the stream to fill your water bottles.

The laptop is halfway charged when you return. You suppose this is good enough and return to the hammock. You write. Then return the laptop to charge once more. Back at the hammock, you take in the afternoon sun and close your eyes.

When they open, it is night, and the cabin door is open again. You blink, and inhale, and listen. This is real. The quality of experience is the only thing to go on, and you know what it feels like to be dreaming, and this isn't it. Right? How can you know when you're dreaming? It's easy to know once you've been awake for a while, but in the moment? How tangible is the quality of reality, really?

You banish the scepticism from your mind. You stand from the hammock and make your way to the open door. The same sterile smell assaults you, stronger now. You take out your phone and turn on the flashlight. Inside there is nothing. Only your things and your laptop, open again.

'What the fuck.' Nobody hears you say it. The night swallows the words. You close the door and turn the lantern on. Shaking, you pick up your laptop and see it is still plugged into the battery, one LED remaining. You unplug the cable and begin to read.

The third act has been broken, though not by you. You can't help but appreciate the storytelling, the finesse of the prose, the way it ebbs and flows, drawing you in and pushing you back. But you hate it. This must have been you; yet you don't remember writing any of this. You aren't sure how you could even end it. It's gotten too dark, too abstract.

You check your watch, the hands read 11:30 and you feel the overwhelming crush of exhaustion. You must have been awake, must have written this, must have just forgotten. The stress. It must be manifesting in physical ways. Losing minutes, hours, lifetimes. The ringing in your ears, except it's not in your ears, it's everywhere, over everything, corrupting the very essence of reality while you must experience it. You must be awake for it.

You are awake now, right? If you don't remember the moment before you doze off, if the continuity of your consciousness has been broken, how do you know who you are? It's the only way to keep that reference, that orientation. If that breaks, how will you find your way back, and what waits for you there?

You wake with the sun and breathe a sigh of relief that the door is still closed, and your laptop is still shut. You reach over and click the button on the battery pack, and the same single LED flashes on. Just one more charge, which you need for your phone. You drink some water and prepare the last of your food. You didn't bring enough for breakfast tomorrow. You sit on the cabin stoop, eating your last meal here and reading what you've written these last couple of days. The sun is still low.

You begin to type, breakfast half-eaten beside you. Lost in the pages, time becomes malleable in the way it only does when you write. You look up, see the full bright of day, and decide to take a break. *A breather would be nice*, you think; a short walk while you recharge.

You stretch and close the door behind you, laptop open next to the sleeping bag. *Just a couple more pages.* You walk to the back of the cabin, to the back of the clearing, down the worn path into the woods. A faint buzzing enters your awareness, but you're elsewhere. You wonder how the story will end. You don't plot. You just write and it always comes, one way or another. The ending always comes. It's part of your craft. What you do is in the moment. It's present and it's real, and sometimes it's even good, but you don't feel good about this story. That itch on your brain, behind your eyes, beneath your skin; that's this story.

The path goes on. It was always there, but all at once the ringing tinnitus engulfs you, penetrates you, and becomes you. There is a bend ahead. You step on. You turn the bend.

The rabbit. Grey fur matted with blood, still bleeding. Somehow more gaunt, more wasted, more gone, but still alive. That piercing gaze holding yours. This shouldn't be, you took care of this. You feel like retching in revolt. You want to turn and run. The desire of your will is pushing against the crescendoing tone of this thing and all the time: the rabbit. Then, all at once, reality crashes back, and you smell iron. You see the blood spilling down the trail, pooling. You feel it sticky and pollocked up your calves, behind your knee, splashing with each step. Revulsion grips you as reality returns, and you breathe. The rabbit is breathing too, ragged and raspy breaths.

You step forward, through the crimson, and sit. Tears well in your eyes, as you reach out and stroke his head. Your wife is beside you; you can feel her warm tears against your chest. You caress his cheek, and your hand comes away with smears of blood from the corner of his mouth. He stares blankly at you, already gone. Burst blood vessels fill his eyes as they dim. He's close now, just skin and bones. He's been sick for so long, and you've been shouldering this for some time. It's almost too heavy.

Your son's chest rises and falls for the last time. The rhythmic beeping of the electrocardiogram becomes chaotic. You finally cry, deep from your core. You hold your wife, and she holds you. The pitchy ring engulfs you both. You hear footsteps approaching from down the hall. They aren't running.

FINOLA CAHILL

TENEBRIS CAPRA

It started when the goat turned black. Purchased three years prior, snow white and stinking, she was no one's favourite but ate the thistle and looked the part. The neighbour's buck had always been black, thus the initial supposition was an open gate. But, when I went to chase the usurper out, there they both were, cud-slow and mawkish, staring at each other across the fence, dark as damp dirt. When the goat shifted its gaze to me, I saw it lacked a good chunk of the tip of the left horn, an asymmetry improbably identical to its missing white counterpart. Gripped between my knees, I ran a hand over its flanks and legs, but no pigment or clay came away under my palm. And, when I peeled the coat into a part, there wasn't a stray white to be found, just chickeny pink skin under black scruff.

I blamed Gurty first, the WWOOFer. She'd been with me near six months now despite only intending to stay for two. Gurty was a fine big woman, good for reaching things on tall shelves, and you could spot the cut of red hair from afar in the fields – a practical advantage. She was a bit German in her ways, but I liked her, on balance. That is to say, I could have extended her a bit of grace, could have been a bit more measured perhaps, in my behaviour. But it wasn't the first thing, you see. The tops of my early-crop potatoes died off, wilting with no kind of blight I'd seen before. When I started digging out the drills to investigate, I'd found the remains of apples in the soil instead, gone to rot, an orgy of pests drunk on the sweetness. Then the neighbour, Tom Óg, he'd dropped me off some sacks of seaweed. I'd hauled them from his boot myself, they were heavy, and smelled fatly of the sea– sulphur and such. Two days later when I opened the bags, hives of flies flew out, unending, deafening, and then gone. Not a piece of seaweed was to be found amongst the sackcloth.

'Gurty,' I shouted, thinking she was away in the fields.

'Naoise,' she responded, popping her head out from the shed but five feet from me.

'The goat!' I said.

'The goat,' she said.

'The goat is black,' I said

'The goat is black,' she said, and smiled. Words warmed in me.

'And have you any idea why the goat might be black?' I said.

She frowned, rolled her eyes, then went back into the shed.

'I said, have you any idea why the goat might be black?' I followed her into the gloom.

She was fixing something, little parts and bolts laid like a jigsaw across her workbench.

'Could you be more particular, please Naoise? What do you think I might have done this time?' She chuckled. 'Why is the goat black,' she repeated, quietly, to herself. She didn't even look at me when she was talking to me. And nothing she said had even the shape of a denial, why, it could have been some prank, or carelessness on her part, and she hadn't even the decency to look sorry or worried. She hadn't said it, but I knew she thought the potato-apples were my fault somehow, my mind going, age tampering with me and all that. And the flies, she said they were probably some foreign locust, come over in an imported house plant. What imported house plant, I said to her. Hadn't I heard about the murder hornets, she said to me. Hadn't I heard about the murder hornets, like I had the time to be reading about beasties outside of my own domain. No excuses for this though, had she? Not a one. No colour-changing goat virus to point at. The wee simmer – the itch in my elbow, in my throat – it chased the word up out of me.

I told her, 'Go.'

She paused, then returned to her tinkering.

'Go,' I said, a bit of a roar on me.

And she did. She lay down her little screwdriver, threw her radish-stained hands up in the air, and went. Back outside I caught sight of the half-hung onions, spade laid prostate beneath them, and went to follow her, but then saw the cat looking at me from beneath the still-damp timber I'd meant to move. She'd had sore eyes for at least a week; I'd bought the drops two days before. I went to open the other shed to search for the box of bits from the vet but instead knocked over a bag of rubbish that was overdue for the tip. By the time I'd remembered to miss Gurty, a full day had passed and it was too late to go after her. The season seemed longer and wetter by the minute.

Tom Óg, a man as young as myself, and myself edging seventy, had been my closest neighbour since I was born. When we were children we were barnacle-stuck to each other, climbing trees, walking to school, pulling pranks – open gates, goose eggs in the hen house and such – and then distracting each other, ripping faces while our fathers roared. We were both alone now. He was one of a heave of sisters, and they'd all married and left. My parents hadn't managed another after me, so the question of who was to have the farm was never bandied about. Neither of us had produced a wife. There was a time when Tom suggested I move up into his house, it was the bigger of the two, and we'd farm the land together, but I'd seen through that land grab. I didn't hear him come in first, but a toe poking out from his sock stuck audibly to the yellowed lino as he crossed the kitchen. He made himself a tea and added the bag to the gasping stack in the sink. Tom was a two-story fella, the head far above me, and his clothes always nicely chosen, good jumpers, pressed trousers, his tidiness a remnant of his life with sisters. The hole in the sock wasn't like him. Standards slipping.

'Well, Tom,' I said.

'Naoise,' he nodded. 'Could do with washing.' He flapped a hand at the polka of dead flies on the sill – they swarmed up from the sink in the mornings and I slammed them against the glass with slipper, book, or hand.

'It could,' I said, 'but sure I've never been known as much of a homemaker.'

He snorted at that.

He'd seen Gurty in the pub four days ago, before she'd managed a lift to the train station. He'd also seen the goat. The goat. I couldn't ignore it. It was there every morning, looking at me from the kitchen window. At first I'd hoped it was a jape, interference from some teenage yoboon sick of smoking behind the swings in town. But when the next dose of heavy rain appeared, the yoke came away still stubbornly black, not even grey. These past four days, I'd checked it every morning for signs of regrowth, for a wink of a white root. I'd even con-sidered talking to the vet, but the story would only turn to pub fodder, I'd be a laughing stock. Anyway, apart from the colour, the animal was unchanged. It came in on bad nights without complaint, knew where to find the left-over chicken feed, and moved from shelter to field, absent of any signs of uncertainty.

'Gurty might come back if you'd only give her a buzz, Naoise,' he said.

'And say what,' I said.

He looked at me over the rim of his mug but made no fur-ther comment. Tom Óg often nosed around my business, but he knew when to leave alone – we were exactly sure of where the fence posts and gates lay between us. I drained my cup and nudged it into a crevice between the eggy breakfast plate and the bean-red dinner pot. Tiny flies seethed from the rift.

'I've my niece for the summer,' he said, and nodded at his house, matchbox-sized from where we stood, a smudge of a girl lying flattish on the hill in front of it. I opened the window to let in the sound of crows.

'She's sick of me, I'll send her over to you sometimes,' he said.

He was already retreating, guilty, like a mutt from the kitchen, scraps in maw. I hadn't time to think of a question, let alone ask it, and he was out the door.

The smell of smoke woke me the next day, thin through the bottom of the bedroom door. I rolled up and out, the sheets held close, and tripped into the kitchen. I saw Copóg first, stretched out in a patch of sun. I'd never seen Tom's dog prone before, although admittedly I avoided the creature as much as I could. It was a rescue border collie, driven mad for lack of work and delivered from town-life a bit too late. Then, I saw the girl. She wore a dress long enough to have been dirtied by the walk over. Her hair was a black plaited stripe, split at the ends but grease-slick at the roots. She was elbow deep in sud, a stack of dishes to her right, a rapidly filling ashtray to her left. I cleared my throat and she turned, looked at me, slowly, a cigarette smoked near to the quick dangling from her lips. The red creep of shame started at the back of my knees.

'I'll just get dressed, and I'll be out. Throw that kettle on.' I backed from the kitchen

Upon my return, she'd made a cup, not a pot, and was sat at the table with a fresh cigarette. The detritus was cleared, and the sink emptied, but a stray butt had made its way to the floor.

'Thanks for the, eh, cleaning,' I said.

She smiled but didn't reply. She could have been sixteen, or twenty-five, the thin lines of her frame seeming even smaller in her oversized clothes. I couldn't for the life of me remember her name, although Tom must have told me. I sat, she stood. The thin purple flowers and sagging waist of her dress seemed alarmingly familiar. Was the child wearing my dress?

'When did you get here?' I said.

Copóg let out a drilling growl.

'A few days ago, a change of scenery for the summer.' Her voice was thick, as though her throat needed clearing.

Had she been in my room? Or had I gotten rid of that dress? It had been my mother's. I looked for a recognizable stain, or rip.

'I came here once before, when I was young, and I liked it,' she said. She put a stack of plates up in the press, then hopped onto the counter, her skirt – my skirt – sopping up the residual soap and water. 'I heard you needed a hand.' She met my eye.

I considered refusing her, tried to collect excuses from the half-cooked trough of them inside me. The dress felt like a threat hung out to dry on the lean angles of her shoulders. But, she was already here, and she'd already seen the kitchen – sure, she'd already cleaned it. And couldn't I use a hand about the place? Gurty's absence had me up at dawn and still not getting it all done. I made for the door, Copóg snarling as I passed.

'Right so. I've an onion bed half-emptied. The rest need to be pulled and cured, they can be hung out over here–'

When I turned to point out the particularities of the shed lock, I realised she had not followed me. She was still on the counter, looking out the window towards the trees. She jumped down, and strode past me.

'I don't do digging. Or vegetables. I'll clean a bit and mind the animals. I saw the geese are still in. I'll let them out.' It didn't seem as though she needed any confirmation from me, so I said nothing. The onions despaired.

I didn't see her again until the fires. I heard her sure enough, and the telltale Marlboro smoke permeated the house. But I'd lie abed, still, listening for her whistle to the dog and the banging door before I'd rouse myself. I'd find the tea bags in the bin, flies wiped from the window, and dishes put away. But a fine tensor of ash built on the floors and surfaces, and cigarette butts congregated in bowls and corners. During the day I'd stick to the crops, letting her away with the livestock. I couldn't complain in that regard; they were all where they were supposed to be in the evenings and none looked to be losing condition. That goat though. The creature had grown secretive, hiding amongst the canopy at the edge of the field, its coat camouflaging it in the thicket of trees. I wanted to ask her to move it to a different pasture, out of sight, but that would've meant talking directly to the girl. I left her out a note, but found it in the bin that evening, and the goat unmoved.

She took to pawing through my things unapologetically. I found old boots pulled from the back of the hall closet and left to air by the stove. One morning, I saw my mother's cookbooks were taken down from the back shelf, dusted, and left open on the table. I found a set of badminton rackets, which I was sure had been under my bed, submerged in the overgrowth of the front lawn, the bag of six shuttlecocks empty beside them. I saw one or two caught, like Christmas baubles, in nearby trees, then found another in the chicken's water, and spotted one more in the distant jaws of Copóg. I dreaded finding the last of them, but couldn't tell you why. The whole thing was irritating. Each unearthed item, each displaced piece of the house – it felt like a hand on me, like a fingerprint's grease, like I might wake up one morning and find myself aired out in the hotpress, or strung up on the line if the day was fine. I knew I should have said something from the off, sure I still didn't know if that was my dress or not, but now the growing height of the accusations paralysed me. And didn't Tom Óg think he was doing me a favour? It was easier to wait it out, I told myself, though the balance between the discomfort of confrontation and the remaining length of the summer was fragile.

One evening, I found my father's wedding ring in a soap dish by the sink, solid gold, forever slightly dinted on one side by a gumming babe. My fingertips felt cold; I imagined it disappearing down the throat of the kitchen drain, and the see-sawy inner debate collapsed entirely to one side. I sat down and dialled Tom's number, then hesitated. My head was all choked. I found a biro and tried to make bulletpoints of what I wanted to say – the moved belongings, she'd never told me her name, the ring, ignored my notes, the feckin' dog is a danger to us all, smoking, fucking ash, everywhere. I was nearly ready to ring him, so I was, then I heard it. A sibilance, snakeish, rising in crescendo and pitch, building to something fraught. Sound emptied and the room lit up, a burst which was neither white nor bright. I ran to the window and saw the fields in front of me patterned with tiny fires, symmetrical, knee height, and evenly spaced. Impossible. A bit aways, across the field, there was the dog, and herself, watching, the fine geometry of her face illuminated by the flickering night.

I ran out the door and through the farm, opening each of the sheds, stables, and hutches, allowing the animals an escape route should anything further catch.

'Hup!' I said, 'hup hup outta there,' I yelled through the open doors. The livestock were nonplussed, although some ambled out into the night, nosing the ground for dropped feed.

The doors and latches were wet to the touch. It had been raining for days, weeks. Although I could see the burning, the smoke smelled pale, like a memory of fire. The farm was quiet except for the echo of my own voice. When I reached the paddock with the boundary fence to the neighbour's land, the goat was nowhere to be seen. It, at least, in its proximity to the incident, had had the good sense to flee. The girl sat on the gate, as unmoved as the rest of the living things of the farm.

'Alright?' she called.

I shrugged, soused in sweat, the heat unbearable. Even if I'd had the words, my throat was shut tight with thirst.

'Strange,' she said, smiling.

I left her there, and went to search for the goat – it couldn't have gone too far.

The fires burned until dawn, and left evenly spaced ashen rounds across the fields. The firemen, who arrived at noon the next day, had a hard time understanding how there had been a fire at all. No accelerant found, the land heaving with moisture, a howling wind that had never stopped, and yet the blackened mark of each fire showed perfect inertia, like tiny hearths.

'It's almost like–' one fella started.

'It's almost like the grass just went black, like it didn't burn at all,' the other finished, scratching the exposed strip of skin between the waistband of his trousers and his bunching t-shirt.

'But the ground is still hot, like,' said the first fella. They both looked at each other, bewildered, and then back at me. Sure enough, when I crouched down and placed my hand to it, the blades of grass, although jet black, were still full and waxy to the touch, not even crisped at the edges.

Once the firemen had eventually left, I rang the neighbour.

'Look it, Tom,' I said.

'Well, Naoise, how–'

'I won't be needing the girleen's help no more, she's done enough now.' I said.

'The girl–?' he started.

I was going to explain, pull up the bullet points, so I was, but then the fatigue stole the fight from me, and all I wanted was the bed.

'Great job, a big job done here on the place. Cleaning, and all.' I just wanted her gone.

'But, di–'

'Yep. A grand job altogether. Sure the worst of the season is over now. I'll call if I need a hand with the late-crop potatoes.' I said without taking a breath, and hung up.

It felt like weeks since I'd had a proper sleep, and the bones of my body seemed to move against each other in new ways as I walked down to the house. I was just through the door when I remembered I should have asked about the fires. I made myself phone him back, and he answered after a single ring.

'Listen, Tom, did you take any damage in the fires?' I said.

'Fires?' he paused, 'what fires?'

'Did you not see the fires? Did the girl not tell you, sure she was out there watching last night like it was feckin' bonfire night.'

'This is it, Naoise, I was trying to tell you, sure herself went home last week, did she not come down to say goodbye to you?' he said.

I thought: well, Tom's finally lost the plot, up there alone in that house all the time. I didn't say it though. I just said, 'Oh!'

'She never mentioned going over to you at all, actually,' he said.

'Oh,' I said, and hung up.

I couldn't find the goat. Neither the evening feed, nor the ache of the heavy udder brought her back, and by the third day I started to look for a carcass. By the third night, I had walked the full perimeter of the land, and found the boundary unbroken, and gates firmly shut. I fell into the close sleep of fatigue, but woke with a start, the unmistakable waft of cigarette smoke pervasive in the room. I was out of bed and through the door instantly, but no one was in the kitchen. The door was still locked, the plates undisturbed in the sink, and the stack of tea bags had started to regain prominence.

I shivered. The morning air had a sharp turn to it – what time was it? I considered returning to the warm cocoon of my sheets, but when I checked the clock it was nearly nine. There was something wrong with the light though. It seemed crowded, lacking in a saturation I hadn't known was there before. Through the window I did not see day, or night, or the something else of the gloaming. I could not see the road, or the steady climb of the hill, or the neighbour's house, or the goat (white or black). Vegetation, heavy and slick looking, had climbed and encircled the land. Vines as thick as thighs wrapped nearby tree trunks, the trees themselves gathered in crowded lines like cavalry, and the blackberry bushes – they had grown years in moments, woven into deadly blankets, unripe fruit a menace. I pinched my arm. Was I even awake? I still smelled smoke. I pinched my arm again, harder this time. I tried to breathe in through my nose and out through my mouth, but my lungs wouldn't fill all the way, could there be something wrong with the air too? I opened the door, forced the hinge of my jaw open as wide as it would go, panting, almost trying to swallow the oxygen. Little white dots crossed by vision. I bent over. I tried to count to ten. I returned to the kitchen, turned on the tap – no water. My throat felt papery, ready to rip. Then I saw the vines advance, in unison, as though a hidden general had commanded it from afar. One fingery tendril curled its way around the doorframe, like a neighbourhood cat.

I ran out, a hare from a form, barefoot. I turned and grabbed a shears from the shed and headed straight for where the gate should have been. As I approached the hedge walls, they heaved slightly, as though in breath. I paused, my mind blank, but then my body resumed motion. I extended the shears in front of me, and charged. I was about a metre away when my left foot, expecting ground, met nothing. My whole body tipped forward over a new edge. I closed my eyes, accepted the drop, but instead felt myself jerked back by the collar, and pulled up from the brink of what I now saw was some kind of moat. Water swirled beneath me, black and cold, punctuated with the threat of undulating, oblong shapes.

'Well, that was close…' she said, and exhaled a giggle.

The wrongness of the light didn't look wrong on the girl. The grey glare liked her skin, and the dark glint of her plait, and the folds of her dress, and the black and white dog at her feet.

I backed away, sheers now pointed at her chest.

'Stop, stop now. That's not going to make you feel any better, is it?' she said. I thought about it, I did, and then lowered the shears, and myself, to the ground.

'What happened?' I asked. A single bead of sweat broke off from my hairline, its path down my face felt like a spider's touch, but I didn't raise my hand to wipe it away.

'Things change.' A description as simple as it was absolute.

'Can they change back?' I took in the scene, a day devoid of birdsong, of rummaging feet, greasy leaves climbing to create a dome above us. She sat down with me, legs folded neatly. She looked so young.

'You ignored the signs. You neglected this place. But you do still have a choice. I can help you get out. We can forge a bridge and you'll cross the waters and I'll tip the log after you and live here alone. But the world beyond here, it's not what it was either, that's all gone now. And this land, if you leave, there's no coming back.'

'I can't leave,' I said. This was my land, my parent's land, the land that holds the bones of generations of good dogs, and the promise of next year's crop, and the place where I broke my arm, and the lost necklace my nan gave me for my communion. I tasted bile. Thick layers of cold settled in on my skin.

'Oh?' she said.

'This is my home,' my voice sounded off, like a recording.

'It's just a place,' she said

'They're all just places,' I said, with more feeling than before.

'There's no changing your mind. In an hour, those vines will be too thick to cut through, and we will be an island, a fortress, a kingdom.

We sat silently then, for a time. I combed through the events of the past weeks, feeling like I had my fingers in a barrel of ropes that needed winding and I couldn't find the start or end of any of them but then my mind ceased to race. And now, I am fixed on a Tuesday early in the summer, a day mundane in its hard sun and sharp breezes. I reseeded the front field without issue, Gurty made something tasty with the ends of last year's jarred beetroot, and I was wrecked, but sated. I'd plans to meet Tom for a pint of porter and a quiet evening together. There wasn't a single bit of news on me, but I knew it didn't matter to him. Home, infinite. Are peace and permanence synonyms? Is stasis sanctuary? I feel the vines on my wrists already, although they were nowhere near touching distance yet. Better the beast you know, my father always said.

I nod to the girl, certain, but then pause.

'Wait,' I say, 'the goat. She's been missing for three days.'

Her mouth grows wider, pinkish in the gloom, and she throws herself upon me, smelling sweet and sour like old hay, palms warm, tacky against the nape of my neck.

'I knew you missed me.'

SOFIE DE SMYTER

YOU'VE GOT TO GET THEM OUT BY THE ROOTS OR THEY'LL KEEP COMING BACK

April 2021

You're absolutely right. The garden isn't much of a garden. *Yet*. But it has everything it needs to become one. The best you've ever seen: plenty of air, dirt, water. And you! Nothing like the imagination of the young.

I get that you'd prefer a nice lawn over this upturned dirt. Totally get it. It's almost summer – love having a barbecue myself. The good news is that you don't need to wait for a garden anymore. Look, I brought some quotes for lawn turf – delivered and put in place – only takes about six weeks for the grass to settle.

I know, incredible, right?

Put some potted plants on the terrace and voilà. Barbecue season can start. And if you feel like it, maybe next year, put in some bushes – plant a couple of trees – one for every baby! It's a four bed/two baths after all.

The tree right next to the terrace? A weeping willow I was told. I wouldn't get a willow, though – for the babies, I mean – short lifespan, willows. You wouldn't want to jinx it. Go for something robust. An oak. Lasts centuries. I mean, bar diseases and the like. Humans.

No, the willow's not dead; it's been pruned to allow the light in through those gorgeous French windows. Plus, you wouldn't want the leaves blocking your drain pipes.

I'm sure you'd rather have the willow removed entirely and save yourself the trouble of having it pruned every couple of years. Don't know why they didn't do it – probably some climate activist!

I know! But as the tree's this bare already, I bet you could cut it to a stump yourselves. Wouldn't try and get the whole thing out, roots and all, I mean – might ruin the terrace. But who doesn't like a good stump? An original feature, if you like. What's the name of that game again? A drinking game, Austrian, German… the one who's slowest at whacking their nail into the stump loses and has to buy the others a drink?

It *is* called "stump"? Love that. Count me in! And once you're done whacking, the little ones can use the stump for a table. Tea-time, play-doh. Can you picture it?

September 2021

You're right. The turf should have settled by now – usually takes no longer than six weeks.

No, I do believe you did everything by the book, ma'am.

Our book, yes. It happens, not often, that turf is rejected – a bit like a transplanted organ. I was just wondering… that tree you were cutting down when we were over? That was a weeping willow, right?

Willows are known for their shallow roots, aggressive little fuckers too – it's possible the roots are preventing the turf from settling. Pushing it back up.

No, I'm not saying you're to blame. The firm that renovated the place should have taken care of that. *Before* they did the terrace. Also, didn't they remove a couple of outbuildings?

Bet they took away some of the dirt while they were at it. They should have replaced it but not everyone's as meticulous. Tell you what, ma'am, we'll provide you with new lawn turf and a top layer but you'll have to talk to them about the dirt. You'll want those roots properly covered this time. I mean, the idiom's six feet under for a reason, right? Bodies. Trees. Tomato *tomato* if you ask me.

January 2022

Yup. Looks like you've been shitting and pissing into the soil these… how long have you been living here?

9 months? Hm.

No, you're right, mate, that does sound unlikely. But I'd say you've been shitt– Well, for quite some time, at least. Hence the smell. And the blockage. But, silver lining: you've got yourself some extra fertile soil. Looks like this place could use it. What are your plans for the garden? Bit of a gardener myself.

What's that?

Focus on the pipes, gotcha!

It happens more often than you think. Renovators rarely bother with the sewage system. Electricity, sure, but not poo and pee. Sometimes it's even the builders who break one of the pipes, but you'd have noticed sooner. I'm betting it's that… well, stump.

You cut it down when you moved in? Yeah but trees are strange creatures alright. Been reading that book by that German fella, whatshisname, some forester. And I'm telling you, trees are the shit!

No? Nothing? Anyhow, what I wanted to say. You know when people die and their hair and nails continue to grow? Same with roots. And the roots of willows don't go deep but wide. That's why they should be planted at least 50 feet away from any underground lines or pipes. I mean, whoever built this house. Not the sharpest tool. Who owned the place before you?

Yeah, I do remember it standing empty for years – but looking at the size of the tree I bet the tree was here first.

They told you the tree wasn't older than 30 years? Bullocks. I mean, willows don't usually grow old, but looking at the rings. Anyhow, this book talks about the "wood wide web." It's like... trees of the same species link up their roots to communicate and to warn each other of danger. Insects. Huge chainsaws–

No? She laughed! I knew she could. But seriously. When one tree's in trouble, other trees help out. This German fella even found a stump that still had life in it after – don't know how long, turns out other trees had been keeping it alive! Sometimes trees even grow back.

Well, you're right, you don't have any other willows – no trees whatsoever – but there's that bit of woodland across the street.

Yeah, true. The roots would have pushed up the street by now but tarmac can cover a lot! And maybe there used to be a whole forest here, of willows. And they're still communicating underground! People always worry about what's going on behind their backs but really, they should worry about what's going on underneath their feet. In the book–

I've been in sewer repair for 25 years, why?

I see. Funny, yeah. Hadn't heard that one before. No, the fumes are not known to cause hallucinations. Fainting, yes. But we never go in without a mask. How long would you say you've been inhaling these fumes?

September 2022

So what you're saying is that the new lawn turf did catch on but that it's full of weeds this time? Ma'am, we put in that turf months ago, and I'm quite sure we'd have had other complaints by now. Your turf comes from a large lot, you know. Besides, our dirt's top quality. If I remember correctly, you live across some woodland, right? I'd say it's more than likely that's where the weeds are coming from.

Sure we can treat the weeds – we have some powerful weedkillers here, but you'll have to avoid walking on your lawn for at least a week. Keep the kiddie in.

No kiddie? Oh, but I was sure you were – quite ready to pop even–

Yes, my apologies, none of my business.

Yes, you'll have to keep the cat inside. I mean, a cat's even smaller than a–

Well, if you won't be able to keep the cat in, and seeing as you're quite attached to it, the only thing I can advise you is to get yourself a good weed puller. If you pull them out with your hands you'll never manage to pull out the roots. And you need to get them out by the roots or they'll just keep coming back and back and–

Yeah, we seem to keep coming back as well, but this really should have been the last time.

October 2022

I want to make sure I'm getting this right: the husband was abroad for two weeks, on business he says, got home this morning and found his wife on the floor, unconscious? Tried waking her, slapped her in the face etcetera, no joy? Then he remembered she'd had a weeding frenzy? Had sent him a picture the day before of a small wound on her left hand. A blister of some sort? Apparently too thick – his words – to know you need to wear gloves when gardening?

He decided to take a look at her hand, saw red stripes all over her palm, spiralling out from the wound. Pulled up her sleeve, noticed how the stripes united in one big red line running up towards her armpit.

And as the wife had spread the weeds all over the floor of the unused nursery – some with roots almost reaching from wall to wall – it's only natural he thought the severely infected wound was an imprint made by one of those weeds. It makes *total sense* to think she'd fallen asleep with her hand on one of the weeds and lost consciousness.

Except the weeds were not weeds. He Google-lensed them and discovered they were willow saplings. And then Google suggested he sell them and he thought that was just brilliant because the roots looked like they would thrive just about anywhere. Even in the nursery where...

Well.

Good thing he got home when he did! That they have a decent Wi-Fi-connection! If he'd Google-lensed the weeds instead of his wife's arm any longer, she'd have been dead – we were just able to stave off full-blown sepsis.

February 2023

You sure you're not pulling my leg? Seen a lot of mould before but nothing quite like this.

It has the look of mould alright – I'll give you that. Heck, it even feels like mould, but I'm telling you, mould doesn't grow in the shape of a weeping willow and, forgive me for saying, but it does look like you're a bit of a fan.

Uh-huh, yeah, it would indeed be weird to have a willow tattooed on your hand, and in red ink at that. Is it a burn?

Might be mould allergy, you know – some people develop rashes. Also, if you've been inhaling the spores for some time they can even start layering up inside; I heard a story about a guy who had a tree growing inside his–

Sure I know the plumber. Why you asking?

Ah, I see.

No, you indeed don't look like you're pulling my leg.

Or like you'd want your baby to sleep in a room full of mould. When are you due?

Oh, I'm sorry I just figured, what with this clearly being a nursery – the crib, rocking chair, and you, well.

No I shouldn't have just assumed. It's a nice room alright – I like the yellow wallpaper, gives the place a sunnier vibe. A baby will be very happy here one day. And overlooking the biggest chicken coop I've ever seen! A whole lot easier to maintain than a garden.

No eggs? Maybe they just have to settle? Some chickens take a looooong time before they–

Yeah, sure, we can get rid of the mould, figure out its source. I'm guessing it's the drainpipe. I know the house's a total makeover but they often don't bother with drainpipes. Looking at that humongous stump down there I wouldn't be surprised to find a whole lot of mulch and leaves. Also: if you want to avoid leaves blocking your drain pipes in the future, I'd take care of the saplings you've got…

Yeah, right there, next to the stump, over by the terrace – did you clear out all the twigs when you got rid of the tree? If you didn't, what you've got there is a nice set of clones. Willows don't need much to–

You alright? Miss?

February 2023

It's just us, Emily! You were dead right to tell me to bring a couple of torches – how long has this blackout –

What's that she's saying? A week?
Surely that's not possible.

No, I'm not talking to you, Emily. Or myself. I'm talking to Joshua, my intern.

Okay, honey, keep your pants on. Well, don't keep them on, that baby has to come out somehow. I'll tell Joshua to stay downstairs.

Makes sense she's not fond of men right now. I heard the
husband left, and that after all their trouble conceiving.
You're quite right – it does smell like a forest in here. After
a downpour. Check if you can get a fire going in that
fireplace, if not for the warmth then for the light. It
looks like there's plenty of wood. Are those – are those
floorboards? Honestly, some people just...

No, still talking to Joshua. But coming up now. Don't you worry, honey, you and your baby will be right as rain. Now where are you?

Oh sorry, let me shine my torch the other way. That's an impressive drawing of a willow you've got on that wall! Very similar to the ones you've got out in the back. They weren't here last time, were they?

Fast-growing? Well, they do say age thwarts your experience of time. But aren't they *very* close to the terrace and the house? I mean, with the wind, it almost looks they're about to reach in–

Sure, I'll close the curtains. Why's this floor so – sticky? What's left of it, anyway. Is that why you started removing it? You spilled something?

I know your waters burst. That's why I'm here, love, but, usually, amniotic fluid is not this... gluey. I mean... it's like, syrup – resin. Also, why didn't you tell me you were pregnant again?

You haven't had sex in a year? Uh-huh. Okay. You're sure you want to stay on the floor, love? I could call Joshua up and we could take you to your room.

You can't get up.

Let me take a look. Hm. Okay. The veins in your legs do indeed seem to have grown into the floor. Literally. I've seen my fair share of varicose veins but these are quite – spectacular. It's rather hard to tell where *your* veins end and the floor's begin. You do know you're supposed to keep moving when you're pregnant, do you?

The floor? No, doesn't seem strange to me. Incomplete, but not strange. I mean, it's a regular hardwood floor, isn't it?

That's indeed not all that regular. Original's the word I'd pick. Eco-friendly. I mean, not many people would go to the trouble – and expense – of recycling a tree for their nursery floor. But why remove it after all–

Slow down–

So what you're saying is that, three weeks ago, you found your husband in here, the veins on his forehead grown into the floor–

> *Joshua, can you check if the emergency services are on their way?*

Nononono, I do believe he fell asleep on the floor. Drunk. That he ripped out the floorboards. Men, booze, temper. Seen it all. I also believe you haven't seen him since. But why do you think he's dead?

Because he freed himself of the floorboard that had grown into him. Uh-huh.

Okay, okay, don't worry – I won't cut you loose. Tell me, how long have you been sitting here?

A week. Okay. And you haven't had anything to eat or drink?

The floor's feeding you. The mother tree is? Uh-huh. Sure.

And it has absorbed your dead husband so you're also feeding on your husband. Okay. Let me stop you right there. We haven't seen any corpses. I mean, we haven't checked the entire house but there would have been a smell. I mean, there *is* a smell. But it's a foresty smell – very much alive. Also: a corpse really does take longer than three weeks to decompose. Even in humid circumstances! But I can't deny you're positively blooming.

What do you mean, Joshua, the ambulance can't find the place? You sure you gave them the right address?

Let me just make sure the baby's... if you could spread–

You did? Well, call them again and then go out and wave them down!

I'll try and get past these veins without them–

What do you mean you can't find the door? Are your eyes open, Joshua?

Going in. This might feel a little... and I'm–

What the hell–

April 2027

You're absolutely right! The house isn't much to look at. *Yet*! But it has everything it needs to become a home. A foundation, for starters! Couple of walls. And you! Nothing like the imagination of the young.

Destroyed by a fire, yes. The chimney hadn't been used in a long time and there must have been a nest in it – twigs, leaves, who knows. Maybe an entire tree! And after that, nature just took over. I mean, look at that garden. Well, woodland, really. But I'm sure you can tame it into a lovely garden. The land's definitely fertile!

You were told bones were found?!

No! I mean, maybe the bones of a couple of chickens or cats. Your regular pet cemetery. But definitely nothing human. The couple who bought it before you – well, I could have told them they wouldn't last. I mean. They wanted lawn turf–

I know! No patience. Happens so often. People get stars in their eyes but then realise a garden's more than they can handle.

Absolutely. The house has been sitting empty for some time, but it indeed looks like they didn't do a single thing to cultivate the garden. I know they had plans but I'm starting to wonder if they were ever here at all. They planned on removing the weeping willow, for one, but they certainly never got round to it. And now – how many are there? You'll need to get rid of them before you start on the house, but once they're gone – I can just picture it.

ELLA BARRON CARTON

THE
DOGSITTER

The garden was the best part of the house. It held none of the darkness, dust nor mustiness that the rest had. It was also the only part of the online profile that was even remotely accurate, and it was what had drawn me there. There were three distinct sections of the garden: the kitchen garden, the flower garden and the orchard. The latter was separated by a thick limestone wall teeming with little blue and yellow wallflowers. Ms Coughlan said the gardeners would be coming by twice a week and that it would not be my responsibility to take care of anything outside. My only responsibility would be to mind the five large wolfhounds and water the few houseplants. There were even housekeepers in three times a week so I wouldn't even have to wash my dishes if I didn't want to.

I followed Ms Coughlan as she showed me slowly around the house, pointing at rooms with a shrivelled and heavily jewelled hand, declaring 'the dogs may roam freely there,' or 'neither you nor the dogs should cross that threshold' interchangeably. I tried to remember which was which, since all the white wooden doors looked the same from the long hallway. This tiny ancient woman I was following around was to summer in Paris with her older sister, and wouldn't be back for nearly three months.

The tour ended in the kitchen garden, with the wolfhounds panting under the heat of their woolly coats and the muggy overcast June day. Ms Coughlan ruffled the head of the oldest-looking wolfhound as she spoke, 'The dogs are allowed in the gardens all day, they know not to dig up any of it, and to undertake all evacuations on the large green at the front, which the gardeners will clean if you don't spot them in time. Please do be mindful of Terry, he has gotten a taste for the blueberries but they make him very ill. And finally, do not under any circumstances let them out on a clear night. In fact, it may be best to keep them in every night if you are unsure about how clear it is going to be. They have beds in the conservatory.' I had seen these beds, large feather-stuffed tartan pillows under the windows. It smelled distinctly of wet dog, which was unfortunate as I thought I would happily spend a lot of time in there otherwise.

Ms Coughlan left that evening in the back of a large black Rolls Royce, driven by a man whose outfit looked straight out of Downton Abbey. He packed up her large tapestry bags as she stood in her pink pantsuit and lace gloves, saying an individual farewell to each of the dogs. It felt wrong to be watching this tender goodbye, and so I stared at the swaying of the trees along the driveway instead; the flickering green looked so dark against the overcast sky.

After she left, I tried to befriend the dogs, but they seemed to have no interest in me. I feared I would have to wrangle them all together soon for their evening walk. The dogs had a strict and detailed routine, and I couldn't help but wonder if delicate Ms Coughlan walked them for seven total miles every day as I was to.

I chose a guest room that overlooked the flower garden, and unpacked my small suitcase. It occurred to me how many questions I should have asked, about washing my clothes and locking up the house if I was to leave. The only contact information I got for Ms Coughlan was for the concierge in her sister's building in Paris.

Once I took out their leashes, the dogs gathered quickly, and I was pleasantly surprised by how well-trained they were. I had to do very little but try and keep up as the dogs walked me around the perimeter of the country house. The online profile had only snapshots of the kitchen, the garden, and one of the guest bedrooms, making it seem like a well-kept albeit average old rural house. The vastness of the estate I now found myself on was confirmed by the dogs, who dragged me through gaps in hedges into a large meadow, where the vibrant primary colours of cornflowers, poppies, and buttercups lit the world. Some of the dogs began leaping, trying to catch butterflies in their sharp jaws; others sniffed and pissed every few centimetres.

At the other end of the meadow, the dogs jerked me into a wood. I couldn't tell if this was part of the property, but the trees seemed to be native and ancient, not like anything I'd seen before. As I stumbled over hidden roots, getting snagged on thorns and branches, squishing damp moss and fungi underfoot, I thought of all the commercial forestry I'd seen over my life. The strict lines of sitka spruce trees growing spindly and quick, blocking all light from the forest floor. How I enjoyed walking there on the weekends if I could get away from the city for a while! Whatever degree of magic I had felt from those forests now seemed depressing, having been dragged through this other, real wood, teeming with life I could sense if not see.

The dogs stopped dead by a large fallen tree, and began sniffing the air, taking careful steps backwards. I took the opportunity to catch my breath and wipe the sweat off my face with the back of my arm. The fallen tree had dragged up a chunk of earth with its roots, leaving a deep gash in the forest floor. There were no dead leaves or plants in the hole; it must have been recently knocked.

I watched as all the dogs' ears pricked at once, and suddenly they were off again, taking a hard right and nearly pulling my arms out of their sockets. We crashed through the undergrowth, birds taking off from every tree we passed. A twisted knot of laurel slowed the dogs down slightly before they ducked below the thick green wall and disappeared. I was yanked forward over a low branch and landed hard on the ground. Instinctively, I let go of the leashes, and lay in the dirt for a moment, suddenly very sure that Ms Coughlan wasn't the one to normally walk her dogs.

I crawled through the gap in the hedging where the dogs had disappeared, and found myself at the edge of the flower garden. The dogs were lolling by the water feature in the centre, panting but otherwise calm.

That night, the thick layer of clouds made it seem a lot darker than it actually was. The western sky showed no change in colour as the sun supposedly set, and I watched the dogs sniff around outside, unbothered. I gathered some fresh lettuce leaves from the kitchen garden, and had a salad for dinner with garden radishes, sugar snap peas, and green onion. The kitchen was well stocked, mostly with fresh fruit and vegetables I'd seen growing by the back door. There was an order book by an old landline, and I got the impression that Ms Coughlan usually kept a cook. After I ate, I opened the conservatory door and all five dogs dutifully trotted in to their overfilled food bowls.

The wind seemed to pick up that night, and I lay under the thick feather duvet listening to the groaning of the old house.

The following days followed a very similar pattern; I woke up early to feed and walk the dogs around the meadow. After this, we let each other off, and I sat in the muggy garden, breathing in the smell of the roses and reading the romantasy book I had brought with me. I ate fabulously fresh lunches, watered the houseplants, and spent more time wandering around the flower garden until I knew the names of every plant. The peonies and carnations were my favourites – shades of pink as bright as plastic Barbie paraphernalia from my childhood, and peaches so soft I wanted to find a way to make blush out of them. Every now and again I saw the gardeners, who were friendly but quiet, and answered my questions about the stranger, more twisted-looking flowers. I would then walk the dogs in the evening, make myself food, feed them, and either take a bath in the claw-foot tub or go straight to sleep.

The dogs seemed happy to stay inside at night, and I decided not to test Ms Coughlan's cryptic suggestion.

As June came to a close, the humidity rose until it was almost unbearable. My clothes stuck to me as the dogs and I walked lethargically around the meadow. They hadn't dragged me into the woods since our first outing, but as the cumulative heat of June pressed down on us, they turned towards the cool dark of the woods. I felt instantly better as we trudged through the undergrowth in roughly the same direction as we had before. My skin pricked with goosebumps as sweat cooled. The dogs sniffed and pissed as they always did.

We came to where I'd expected to see the fallen tree, but I must have gotten turned around somehow. Instead there were six very large, very ancient trees, with some smaller saplings poking up all around. There was one oak that must have been the widest tree I'd ever seen. As I stared up, I was unable to see the canopy. The dogs stood cagily behind me. The shade of the tree was so total that I felt like I had stepped out of midsummer and into midwinter. I wanted to lay my head against the moss-covered bark, to listen to it or hug it, but the dogs began tugging me away. 'Stay! Bad dogs!' I shouted as they kept pulling on their leashes. I piled all of them onto one hand haphazardly, letting the tips of my fingers on the other graze the bark of the tree before I was yanked away again.

We came to a thick stone wall that meant we must be by the orchard. We wandered around the edge of the wall for a while, until we came to a barbed wire fence, separating the woods from another field. The dogs hopped through easily, and waited patiently as I tried to navigate the wire, catching my t-shirt and tearing the seam. We hopped back into the kitchen garden from that field just as it began to rain.

Thick, warm drops of water landed on my arms and back as I bent over to free the dogs. The smell of the rain mixing with hot earth was intoxicating, and thunder rolled above. By the time I got to the kitchen door, I was absolutely soaked.

I took a quick shower and listened to the thunder as I put on moisturiser in my room. The flowers were getting knocked around by the weather, and I could see the roses losing petals near the laurel hedge. A flash of lightning lit up the flat charcoal sky, and I thought about that oak in the woods. Surely that was the tallest thing around, and if the lightning came our way I knew it would be toast. I moved around by the window, hoping to spot it beyond the laurels. Strangely, I could only see a low, monotonous treeline.

I went into another of the guest rooms, with windows at a different angle. Again, the treeline looked flat, with no ancient oak holding court, no five supportive towering ash or beech. I went down the corridor to a different room again, one I had not been in before. The air was thick with dust, and there were white sheets over the furniture, making stout oddly-shaped ghosts. From the window, I saw several tall trees swaying in the harsh wind, with the tallest in the middle. That must be my oak, I thought, considering all the ways the angle of this window differed from the guest rooms.

Downstairs, I let in the sopping dogs, who surrounded me before shaking dirty droplets off and onto my clean pyjamas.

We didn't go out for our evening walk that day. As the rain pelted the thin old panes of the conservatory, the dogs and I watched as the distance between thunder and lightning shrank. I made a strange bean stew with what ingredients were left in the pantry; French beans and green onion, beetroot and carrot. Steam rose from my bowl as I sat in the darkened kitchen.

I fell asleep quickly that night, the sound of the rain scratching some itch in my brain. At some point overnight, the thunder died and the rain stopped. I was woken up suddenly in the dark by the sounds of howling. I tried to cover my ears against it, but when it didn't show any signs of stopping, I hopped out of bed and made my way towards the conservatory.

I didn't bother turning on any lights; the moon was so bright through the window panes it might as well have been morning. The dogs were cowering together, pressed against the wall and staring out the window. The howling continued and I realised it must be coming from the flower garden. I went to approach the window but the dogs bit on to the backs of my pyjama bottoms. I tried to hoosh them off, trying to be gentler with them because of their apparent fear. When I looked up, I caught the glimpse of something white moving very fast across the edge of the garden and into the laurels.

The next morning, the sun was shining on a garden that was truly battered by the storm. There were rose bushes without their petals, and the hollyhocks and evening primrose had all been knocked over, their long stalks snapped at the base. The dogs ran around frantically that morning, peeing on every corner of the flower garden, sniffing and whining and growling at the air.

In the back of the garden, near the orchard, one of the gardeners was staring at a large hole in the ground, maybe two metres in diameter. 'Did you let those damned dogs out here last night?' he asked.

'No, I didn't, they seemed to be spooked by the weather! They stayed in all night.'

'Ha!' he said in disbelief.

I noticed there was no pile of earth near the hole, but the gardener began walking towards the tool shed before I could defend the dogs any further.

The dogs and I went on our morning walk in the meadow. They had no interest in approaching the woods, and neither did I. Instead, the hip-high grass and wildflowers transferred the previous night's rain onto their coats and my shorts. We dried in the sun as we walked back up the lawn, and I could see pungent steam rising from the dogs.

I spent some time helping the gardeners that afternoon. Part of me felt like I needed to make it up to them, even though I had no hand in the storm or the mysteriously large holes. Two more were found in the orchard, and one in the middle of the bed of Juliet Roses. Martin, the head gardener, was heartbroken, as they were his pet project – the rarest type of rose in the world, and just beginning to bloom. I knelt in the soft earth of the kitchen garden and weeded around the onions and carrots, unsure how else to help.

I had never had a garden as an adult, and as a child my parents had tarmacked over the front garden to make an extra car parking space, while they kept the grass in the back short and neat. For over a decade I had lived in apartments and townhouses where nothing grew outside. The best I ever got was one shared house in Kimmage, where a housemate grew mushrooms in their wardrobe, and there was a very floral grotto to the Virgin at the end of the lane. It's not that I never wanted a garden, there just never seemed to be anything in my price range with one that wasn't deep in suburbia. My favourite place that I ever had was an illegal bedsit in Glasnevin, where I shared a toilet with six neighbouring couples and had a mini fridge and a hot plate for a kitchen. It was only a short walk from the botanic gardens, and I spent as much time as I could there, wandering around the glasshouses and watching squirrels run up the trees. It's possible to believe you're not missing out on anything when you just never have it, but as I sat in the baking heat that afternoon, I was no longer so sure.

The sky stayed clear all day, and turned a tabernacle gold as the sun began to set. The dogs were scratching at the conservatory door to get in, even though they had spent most of the evening napping already. Once inside, they began pulling their beds away from the windows, towards the wall where I had found them in the early morning. I had almost begun to believe that blip in sleep must have been a dream, but seeing the hounds cowering again I became concerned. Something large must have been out there last night, and whatever it was, was scary enough to freak out the wolfhounds.

'You have nothing to be scared of,' I cooed, 'you are descendants of wolves, you are the fiercest beasts in all the land.' They continued to whimper and cower, and it took a great deal of effort to slip out of the conservatory without them all following me.

I brought a glass of Riesling out into the kitchen garden to watch the sunset. The bottle had been left open in the fridge, and it tasted disgusting despite being one of the more expensive bottles I had ever tried, a 1990 vintage. The bench was still warm from the day's baking, and I breathed in the smells of lavender and thyme. The sage was flowering and there was a light smell of roses in the air, from where the gardeners had piled up their remains in the compost heap. I sat there with my disgusting wine in the golden evening, wondering if this was joy, if this was what pure happiness felt and smelt like.

The sun finally set, and the air had that clean frigidity that follows a storm. I was picking up my phone and wine glass, ready to go back inside, when I heard a rustling from the flower garden. I padded over to where the hollyhocks had been poorly resurrected, and peeked between their woody stalks. The laurel boundary was quaking and twigs were snapping, but nothing emerged. I walked to the conservatory and peered in, counting the dogs to be sure none had escaped. All five were cowering in the corner together, and when they saw me they began to yelp.

Turning to walk back to the kitchen, I saw it – a large, pure white wolf's head stuck out from the bottom of the hedge. I started running back, hitting the crystal wine glass off the wall, shattering it as I ran. From the kitchen door I saw it fully for the first time, about eight-foot-long with a tail that batted from side to side, causing a rush of wind to move the leaves of the hedge. It cocked its head to one side, looking at me, then stretched towards the sky and howled.

I leapt into the kitchen in a blur, locking the door behind me. I placed the stem of the wine glass on the counter. Out the window I could see it pacing around by the laurels until five wolf pups emerged. I assumed they were pups, even though they were as tall as the wolfhounds currently cowering in the conservatory. Once all had emerged, they began wrestling and playing. I watched in awe as the largest wolf walked around the garden, pissing on full flowerbeds with one stream. The peonies and cosmos, chrysanthemums and alliums were knocked almost prone everywhere the wolf went. The pups dug some holes together, and placed something I couldn't quite make out in them before filling them back up again.

I stared for a long while, until the fear melted from my veins, and I began wondering what their names were, where they came from, why they seemed to be gardening. Their activities appeared to take place strictly in the flower garden, with the largest wolf hopping over the massive stone wall into the orchard every now and again.

Upstairs, I dragged the antique chair over to my bedroom window and slid it open. I could hear the wolves snuffling as they went about their work, the smaller ones taking breaks to tackle one another every now and again. I watched them all night, their white coats glimmering in the moonlight. By the time dawn was breaking, my eyes were tired and my lower back was killing me. Once the first proper ray of sun broke the horizon, the younger wolves began filing through the gap in the ditch. After the last pup had disappeared, the mother looked up at me in the window, cocked her head again before ducking into the ditch.

I awoke to the sound of someone knocking on my bedroom door. I had made it to my bed at some point, although the chair by the window assured me I hadn't dreamt it all up. There was a housekeeper at the door, who looked startled to see me in pyjamas when I opened it. 'Ah, so you are here,' she said, 'I let the dogs out this morning, I was surprised to see them still in the conservatory.'

'Yes, I'm sorry I must have slept through my alarms, what time is it?'

'Noon. It's not good to disturb a dog's routine, you know.'

'Yes, I didn't do it on purpose,' I said, closing the door on her. Out the window I could see the gardeners moving. I quickly got dressed and went down to walk the dogs.

It was another bright and warm day. Clouds moved quickly across the sky, and the dogs traipsed back and forth through the garden anxiously. I took them on a particularly long walk, skipping the woods but circling the meadow a few times. The garden seemed to be doing surprisingly well. A lot of the roses which had lost their flowers in the storm were already beginning to bud, and the gardeners trawled back and forth with lawnmowers and clippers. When I took out the food bin from the kitchen, I noticed that there were a few small saplings on top of the usual garden detritus. I asked Martin where they came from and he said they were growing beneath the apple trees in the orchard, and wouldn't have survived there.

I stayed up late, waiting for the wolves to return. The photos I had tried to take of them on my phone didn't come out at all. I sat in the chair by the window as the sun set. Clouds moved quickly against the darkening sky, but the night on the ground remained still. No wolves emerged.

It was a few drizzly days before I saw them again. The dogs and I fell back into our routine, as though nothing had happened. June stretched into July, and I made small talk with the gardeners and housekeepers about the weather, about the typical Irish summer. We went on our walks, lounged in the conservatory and ate at regular intervals. Food and wine were delivered to the house without my ordering it, some basic list on repeat, and I found I never needed to leave the estate.

In brief patches of sun between showers, I spent time in the vegetable garden weeding and picking out broken glass and stones. Martin showed me how to transplant seedlings into the beds, and I helped sow turnip, radish, and beetroot. The broad beans died back and broccoli was transplanted in their place. I harvested lettuce leaves from plants that had gone to seed and found they were bitter to the point of being inedible. Some of the onions I pulled were rotten and soggy. The first potatoes were small and smooth skinned, and I saw the dogs watching me with curiosity as I dug around in grow bags looking for them.

It stopped raining the day of the first potato harvest, and I decided to eat some outside with pork chops and fresh peas.

I slathered everything in butter, which melted quickly and rolled around the plate as I tried to balance it on my lap.

The dogs were already in, sleeping, and night fell quickly as I sat outside alone. In June, it felt like the sun would never set, but in July it certainly did. This sunset was all peach and pastel blue, and the few clouds above were a bright salmon. When the sun disappeared fully, and I had eaten to bursting, I heard the rustling from the laurel again. I quietly slipped back into the kitchen and put down my plate and glass, and then went back outside.

From the kitchen garden, I watched as the giant wolf's head peered through the small gap in the hedge. We locked eyes and she exhaled sharply through her nose. The laurels shook furiously and parted as she pulled her humongous form out of the woods. She was quickly followed by the five playing pups. The mother watched me for a while, as the pups went about their play and fighting. After a while, she tossed her head to the side, and began walking towards the orchard. I felt like I had won some kind of trust, but didn't push it by trying to get any closer.

I stood there for a long time, watching the pups dig holes together, and placing what looked like little brown rocks in before burying them. The mother went around the flowers, marking their territory and chewing off the dead heads of the roses. As she got closer to me, I saw her white coat was a swirl of spirals.

Eventually, I grew tired and cold, standing so still in the garden, and made my slow retreat into the house. The wolfhounds were whining in the conservatory. On the landing, I made the rash decision to go into the dusty room rather than my bedroom. The moonlight lit the dust motes, and they looked like little will-o'-the-wisps floating in the air.

I made my way over to the window and noticed straight away that the tall trees I'd seen before were no longer there. When I looked down at the flower garden, I saw five glowing child-like figures, with hair made of lichen and moss, clawing at the ground together. One shoved the other, and they all piled on top of the shover, spores or sparks flying off them as they wrestled. A tall glowing woman, with skin like moonlight had wildflowers growing like body hair: daisies and yellow rattle and yarrow and poppies, corncockle and cornflower, hawkbit and vetch. I realised the children had some too, but smaller and lighter. The mother pulled the children apart, and placed an acorn in the palm of the smallest one, before running back towards the orchard.

The next morning, I went out early, before the gardeners arrived but after the wolves had left. The ground seemed even where they had dug holes, and small saplings the size of my index finger poked out. Between the roses, I saw small wildflower buds glistening in the dew.

Each morning after the wolves left, I looked at what gifts they had tried to raise; little elder and hawthorn and birch trees on the grass, crab apple and hazel in the orchard, dandelion and thistle between the roses and beneath the hydrangea. After their second visit, I started bringing the dogs through the woods again, looking for the large trees. Sometimes we found them. Most of the time we returned to the meadow, happy just to have spent any time between the trees.

STEVE DENEHAN

NORTH STRAND SUMMER *seventy–five years ago*

Regrets pile up
over eighty-five years
is what I would have thought

but there is one
that stands above the rest
for my father

he stands in his back garden
summer scabs on his knees
a blue sky above him

*nothing
is more dangerous
than an idle boy*

the airgun feels heavy
in his right hand
not a little boy anymore

he looks up, squints
to see the sky
blighted by imperfection

a small dark shape
straight-line-moving
he points, pulls the trigger

is disappointed
by the retort
not thunderous, but effective

the shape starts to fall
panic-spiralling
a crow, one wing working

one wing limp
my father watches
watches it fall in silence

watches it land
not far from him
with a wet thud

unaware then that the crow
dead as soon as it hits the ground
will live with him forever

DORIAN ROSE

COMPOST

Christine has finished her biscuit. Her tea is cold.

She sits on a wooden deck chair in a garden beginning to bloom, shivering under grey April sunlight. She knows she must rise. It is time to return to the kitchen, to brew another tea and attempt once more to focus on the book in her lap. *A chapter a day*, Pamela has commanded her. *Consistency – that's how a habit's born.*

Christine is retired. Ten weeks, so far, of soul-numbing boredom. She has asked every retiree she knows how they cope, many times over. *You just need a hobby*, everyone has told her. *Something to keep your mind busy.*

Christine has tried them all. Every day for ten weeks, a new hobby – she has tried everything. Violence flashes in her eyes at the barest mention of crochet.

With a sigh, she rises from her seat and retreats through the French doors into the kitchen. There, Pamela slumbers in her seat at the table, head slumped over her own cold brew.

Christine fills the kettle and flicks the switch, watching her wife for signs of consciousness.

The rumble of boiling water rouses Pamela over slow seconds. She sits up, yawns, fluffs her hair.

'Tea, dear?' Christine asks when the kettle quietens.

'Please.' Pamela returns to the dry toast before her as though unaware she was dozing moments before.

Christine glances at the clock beside the fridge. Twelve past eleven: approximately ten more hours until it is socially acceptable to return to bed. She turns her attention to her tea-making duties. Drops a fresh bag into each mug, watching the auburn stain leach through the water. 'Any plans today?' she asks.

'I thought I might visit the garden centre.' Pamela pauses as a second yawn shudders through her. 'The foxes have been ravaging the garden all winter. My daffodils have made it, but I'll be surprised if we've a single summer bulb left alive.'

Pamela has been a gardener all her life. She began in her grandmother's garden at five years of age – Christine learnt this the day they met. Aged nine, Pamela began a secret, likely illegal garden in the woods behind her parent's flat with pansies uprooted from a neighbour's window box. A horticulture apprenticeship at sixteen had launched a career tending the gardens of hospitals, stately homes, national heritage sites and the occasional palace. Six years ago, Pamela retired. They sold their city centre flat to move into a village in the Downs, where she at last had space for a garden of her own – and Christine is sure this is the secret. Pamela has faked retirement. If she runs out of work in her garden, she calls their friends to ask if their gardens are bearing the winter well –

are they quite sure they don't need a second pair of hands? She thought she spied a few weeds beginning to sprout on her last visit.

But Christine cannot fake her retirement. She was a dive instructor, until her health took a turn. Four months ago, she went through a fainting spell and Pamela insisted she visit her GP. An ECG captured an episode of atrial fibrillation. The doctors assured her that, with proper management, the condition shouldn't significantly alter her life expectancy. This management included remaining on dry land, as fainting underwater was considered a threat to her longevity.

Sometimes, she lies in the bath with her ears underwater and plays whalesong through waterproof speakers. If she's gone for too long, Pamela knocks on the door with a cup of tea and a tremor in her voice.

'Don't overbrew it, my love.' Pamela is watching her from the table.

Christine adds milk, commits the tea bags to the food waste bin and sets Pamela's mug before her, taking the seat opposite.

A few quiet moments pass. Christine's teaspoon clinks against her mug as she continues to stir her drink, creating a little whirlpool at the centre.

Pamela looks up. 'I don't suppose you want to join me, dear?'

Christine pauses her stirring. 'Would you mind?'

'If I minded your company, I've made an awful mistake marrying you.' Pamela sips her tea. 'We could go to the little café.'

Something stirs in Christine's breast. Though she has never found joy in gardening itself, she enjoys the garden centre scones. And the dank little aquarium. Fancy goldfish. The miniscule fish with the glowing blue stripes, and all those snails. Perhaps that could help her – a fish tank, to bring something of the underwater world into their home. But would Pamela agree?

Pamela is still watching her. Christine stands, tea in hand. 'I'll take this to the garden,' she nods to the tea. 'I'd better finish my chapter before we go.'

Pamela nods warmly.

Outside again, Christine places her mug on the spare deckchair and shifts her own chair deeper into the sunlight. She sits, pulls a woollen blanket over her knees, and opens her book. Fifteen minutes, perhaps, to drink a cup of tea. She can finish a chapter in that…

'Chris!'

She jolts awake. Reaches out a tentative hand, and finds her tea cold.

'Christine!' Pamela emerges from the kitchen, dressed for the brisk outdoors. 'Dear. Are you coming?'

'Am I coming?'

'To the garden centre? Or am I to replot the entire flow-erbed on my own?"

Christine tries to stand, but her legs are entangled in the blanket. She stumbles free and rushes to the hallway. There, she pulls her waterproof from a peg on the wall: a metallic ombre rainbow. She pulls her favourite scarf from the pocket – pale blue with calicos printed in various poses. She turns to find Pamela looking her up and down.

'Well then,' Pamela says. 'Ready to go?' Pamela's water-proof is maroon, left open to display a beige argyle cardigan and brown corduroy trousers. They're rolled at the hem to show off a few inches of the green vines tattooed along her shins, and combat boots so battered Christine would believe they'd seen real war.

Christine tries to return the same impenetrable once-over, but a burgeoning smile threatens to compromise the effect. She turns away with a nod and makes for her seat in the passenger side of their little green car. Driving, too, is on the list of questionable activities.

Pamela turns the keys in the ignition, the engine sputters to life and they reverse clear of the gravel driveway.

Theirs is the only car on the road this morning. Asphalt winds grey through golden fields of rapeseed bordered by ragged stands of trees. As the car crests the final hill descending towards the garden centre, Christine spies a glimmering band of ocean a mile to the East.

The garden centre is a twelve-minute drive from their house: just long enough for their conversation to stutter, but not so long as to invite despair. It's a low building, half concrete and half glass. Pamela parks the car in the farthest corner of the car park and Christine knows better than to protest. Pamela swears by short walks as a preventative to arthritis, and Christine does not have the mental energy to feign interest in the subject.

'Will we need a trolley?' she asks as they approach the entrance.

'I thought we'd have a look around first, make a list. We can go around again after tea – saves carting everything into the café, or an extra trip to the car.'

Christine considers suggesting the extra trip could be good for Pamela's joints.

She decides against it, and takes Pamela's hand.

Together, they delve through the automatic doors and into the grim gloom of the hardware section, where hoses coil like anacondas about their reels. There is another set of doors at the end of the aisle. The sun blazes through like fire bubbling in a dragon's throat. It is there they will find the potted plants.

The doors slide open at their approach and they step through, into air thick with the fragrances of untold varieties of flowers.

Pamela seems unsure what she's looking for. 'Something to go with the daffodils,' she keeps muttering, still unaware the last surviving daffodils met their end some nights past at the claws of the neighbourhood foxes.

Christine does not enlighten her, for fear she'll be scolded for feeding them. Moreover, if she destroys Pamela's only inspiration, they could be there until the café closes.

She shadows Pamela, trying to understand the garden centre through her eyes. She points to the pansies: 'Don't they look like little lion's faces?' But Pamela is unimpressed.

For several minutes, Christine watches her struggle to read the back of a bag of compost without the assistance of the horn-rimmed glasses hanging from a cord around her neck.

'I think I'll go for a wander,' Christine says.

'Mmm.' Pamela does not look up.

Christine strolls away without particular aim. She finds a set of arched trellises arranged in a circle, hydrangeas creeping along their slats to choke out the light. In the centre of the circle gurgles a water feature, the designer's attempt at a cherub strikingly reminiscent of a gargoyle. And there are gnomes here, lewdly arranged in the shadows by some errant youth.

Christine wanders further, and finds a hedge maze. She tries to lose herself within, only to discover it is no maze but a display of hedgerows arranged in simple lines. They channel her to a low stone wall that marks the boundary of the garden centre. It seems a pleasant place to sit in the sun – perhaps she should have brought her book – until she peers closer and notices a legion of caterpillars squirming over the surface. The hairy, gingery sort that seem... actually, they seem rather charming. She watches them awhile, wondering where they're crawling to. Are the leaves tastier on this side of the wall? She wonders if they're watching her too, pondering what business she has in their territories. She wonders if they have many thoughts. Or eyes.

She begins to feel like a voyeur. She straightens, gazes up at the cloud-speckled sky and cracks her lower back. Just then, a spaceship streaks across the sky.

Christine blinks and grinds her palms into her eyes. Tonight, she will watch the 6 o'clock news and see a recording of a teardrop shaped vessel plunging red through the atmosphere, thrusters blazing every colour of the rainbow. But for now, she believes she has seen an uncommonly bulbous biplane – believes her contact lenses must have shifted momentarily and warped her vision. Or perhaps it's hunger: two hours at least since she has eaten. All the more urgency to retrieve her wife and bear her to the café.

She returns to the daffodil display to find Pamela has moved on. She's with the pansies, eyeing an especially vibrant purple and orange specimen.

'Oh!' Pamela jolts when she senses Christine at her side, nearly dropping the flowerpot. 'Well then.' She returns the pansy to the centre of the display. 'Café?'

'Café,' Christine agrees, and they return to the relative warmth of the interior.

To her relief, there are still scones in the café. She's pleasantly surprised to find a miniature pot of bramble jam. Pamela opts for a safe strawberry, but matches Christine's cappuccino. They take a table by the window and stare out into the carpark. It's a pretty one, as carparks go. Bordered by the boundary wall, and a thin strip of grass rife with fading snowdrops.

'Do you know?' Pamela asks. She dips her teaspoon into her cappuccino's chocolatey froth and begins to eat it like a dessert. Christine takes this as permission to do the same. It takes Pamela a few minutes to consume all her froth, with a thoughtful pause here and there. 'I can't think how long we've been coming here.'

Christine tries to remember. 'We came the month it opened.' Pamela had suggested the date with otherworldly enthusiasm, bouncing on her heels, eyes electric with excitement. It had alarmed Christine at the time. 'I don't think we'd been seeing each other long.'

'We drove in separately, didn't we? I remember your blue Fiat. Hideous thing.'

'Before we lived together, then.'

'Was that the time I was late?'

'You were always late.' But Christine places it then. Her blue Fiat, and mould on the walls of her flat. She'd worried she would smell like damp.

Pamela chuckles. 'You were wearing that cow jumper.'

Christine smiles. They'd found it together in a charity shop the second time they met: a belted Galloway standing in a cloudy sky, they assumed because the knitter forgot to include the ground. 'You were incredibly late.' Christine sat in her dusty Fiat with her boots on the dashboard and waited a full hour with her phone in her hand, thinking this was a strange place to be stood up – but a gentle place. She wouldn't easily be identified as a failed romantic by passers-by.

She gave it ten more minutes, then five, then three, then Pamela appeared. Flower-print combat boots, a grey denim jacket, eyes lined in smokey black like a pirate. *So sorry – lost track of the time – let me pay for your coffee – have you been here long? God, let me get you some cake. Let's get a slice of everything. I forgot my card!* A final apology by way of a triceratops plant-er gifted at their next encounter. A uniceratops now, it still lives on the bathroom windowsill.

'Our fifth date,' Christine concludes, because she's sure it was on the fourth that she decided it was wiser to feign an interest in plants than to risk missing a day out with Pamela. 'You'd just got your leopard print mullet.'

'Thirty-four years ago, I think,' Pamela says.

Christine meets her amber gaze, and the tenderness there brings something out of her. 'They're all dead, Pam.'

Pamela's back straightens. 'If you mean the daffodils–'

'I'm sorry.'

Pamela sighs. 'You can keep feeding the foxes if you must.' She reaches for Christine's hand across the table, though stops short of a reassuring squeeze. 'But you'll be paying for the damage. And we'll replant everything together.'

'I'd like to get a fish.'

Pamela regards her.

Christine finishes her foam in silence, and begins on her scone. She's ravenous. It's gone in a few bites, and she's left to draw out her coffee while Pamela's remains tauntingly whole on its plate.

Pamela looks peaceful, sitting back with her hands cupping her coffee cup, savouring the warmth. Christine tracks her gaze to the trees beyond the boundary wall. She's watching the branches stirring in the wind, young leaves fluttering, or the sunlight spilling golden past the canopy and casting dappled shadows onto the grass. Dewdrops like scattered stars.

'I've been thinking of putting in a pond,' Pamela says. She makes the first cut into her scone. 'We could cat-proof it, if you'd like to put some fish in.'

'Really?' Christine wonders if they'll find any glow-in-the-dark pond fish. She finds herself taken with the thought of an eel. A little Moray, lurking in the rocks. But would it eat the other fish? She could ask the aquarium staff. 'Could we have a fish tank too? In the study?'

'As long as I don't have to clean it.'

'That's what the snails are for. I think.'

'And it's time for kittens, Chris. I've waited long enough.'

SHANE LARKIN

CRADLE

Ben moves the pram along the hollow of a steep hillside, little Pól snoozing gently inside. The day is perfect spring, heaving with life.

The route is familiar now. The same low murmur on the breeze. The smell of milk. The day swirls with it, and with the mad singing of crows in the hills, their voices lancing Ben's skin. He can't stop smiling.

Ben was never a superstitious person, not really. Gráinne was, but in a decorative sort of way. Hazel branches by the door, chrysanthemum petals in corners, in coat pockets. Little gnomes greening in their front garden, standing sentry with a wink. The other locals mostly danced to that same happy tune. Candles and stories for the grandchildren on Imbolc, old songs about love, work, murder, home. Foxes that wail on moonlit nights, scared of their reflection in the waters, they say. That kind of thing. These bits of colour and place crackled merrily among the locals like a turf fire, but that's all it was. A bit of colour. A fine place to bring up children. Ben just followed Gráinne's lead. Not worth taking things more seriously than that.

The hunt for a home had been long and predictably painful. The baby was coming and tensions were rising, tightening, right up to the shoulders. The house was secluded, a poky little two-bed. Everything was far away, hard to get to, but they managed. Could work from home. Flanked by lakes and rivers lost among bogs, big patches of mossland and plant tussle. For now, it was a fine place to be.

It had its issues. Bits of neglect, overgrowth. Mould in the corners that never stayed gone. They needed the electricians in, plasterers, plumbers. But they were getting there. Making it work.

Ben nudges the pram deeper into the glen. Birdsong getting quieter, sinking into the furze. He breathes deep and his eyes go wandering, grazing with the lambs and other things fussing about in the green. A milky tang spoiling on the breeze, the low gurgle of it. Same as usual. His feet don't alter course.

Ben knew pregnancy hadn't been kind to Gráinne. She'd watched other friends going through it and they were luminous, their happy faces, carrying it with a sunny poise. She talked about it with him early on, wanted him to understand. At its worst she felt used, a meat vehicle for some lumpy, kicking thing sapping the colour from her gums. She didn't want to disappear. And the shame of that, the prickling guilt of it. Ben listened. He wouldn't let her disappear. He knew she'd be great. She was the most nurturing person he'd ever known. He thought he'd manage, too. She'd get them through it.

In his memory, the birth itself was all wires, drips, tubes. Urgency noises. Things stayed difficult for the first few months, waiting and healing. Crying, pumping. Trying to nudge the right feelings to the surface, the joy and the love. The proper feelings you were supposed to have. Those feelings did come for Gráinne. Eventually. She made out that they did, at least.

But there was that night the electricity went, a couple of weeks in. The baby, mercifully, asleep and oblivious. The new parents held each other in the candlelight and Gráinne spilled open.

'I don't know what to do. Everything is wrong. I'm barely here.'

She never brought it up again, but the words stayed fixed in Ben's mind.

He swears they still share it sometimes, the waning, in held glances, heavy and slow, like cloud shadows on a rock face.

Ben sees the cloistered thickets ahead. He wonders who else can see them, what it might take from them. But there's no one else around.

Pól stirs. A low croaking in his little chest. Ben takes no notice and sings a happy, tuneless song.

How long had it been since his last visit? Days? A week? He has a look at the land stretched out like an offering around him, the sheep and other little bodies simmering deep in the cauldron of the glen. The warm stink on the air. He moves the pram into tree-shadow.

Ben usually felt the right thing at the right time for the big moments. Proposing. The pregnancy news. Getting the house. Why wasn't it happening now? The baby was here. He was hard work. He wasn't sleeping. He wasn't latching. Why wasn't he latching? But he was here. He had Ben's eyes, every-one said so. Why wasn't he feeling the right thing?

'You keep calling him "the baby"', Gráinne said once. 'Call him by his name.' He apologised, didn't mean it, didn't notice. But of course he did. He was exhausted. Gráinne was exhaust-ed. Tears, milk clogs. Things she wouldn't share. She had noth-ing left for anyone else. There was the baby and whatever sleep she could scratch out of the day. She didn't want to be touched.

He took the baby out for midday walks while Gráinne stole sleep back at the house. He told the baby he loved him when he was with her. He did what was expected. Tamped the rest of it down.

He felt itchy all the time, blistery right under the skin. Raw and bitter. And he felt small. Then, before long, he felt something on the outside. A murmur. In the clammy dirge of a sleepless night, a few months into parenthood, he felt it. Something was there with them in the house.

It became all he could think about. The murmur, the weight, cold and sogging. Curdling the breath in his throat. He didn't know if Gráinne felt what he did, if she was visited in the same way. He didn't know how to put words to it. When he tried to, they fell away like petals in the breeze. He spoke around it. Did she know what he meant? It seemed like she did, sometimes.

After several nights, it was obvious to him. The murmur, what it was saying without saying anything at all. There was a price they hadn't paid yet. *You shouldn't be here.*

Ben moves the pram through the last foraging of afternoon light. There's an early gathering of dusk, wide evening glooms of purple and slate. A temporary shadow. Not far now. His thoughts start to diffuse in the haze as the tree feels closer.

A yelp from Gráinne one night, somewhere between their 2am and 4am alarms. Ben reached out to graze her shoulder. She jerked away. It was her hip. He got her a heating pad and ibuprofen from the kitchen.

'I'm bleeding, too,' she said.

'Bad?'

'Not really. The same.'

They sat together. Pól was crying. Gráinne held her face in her hands, muffling a laugh or a sob. Something spiky and hot.

'What's the secret, then? What do you want?' she said to no one in her dead-of-night voice.

'Come here to me,' he said in his.

'I don't want a fucking hug, Ben. Please. I'm sorry.'

And it hung there, the moment, her question, taut like tripwire between them.

Ben got to know some locals on his strolls with the baby. He met a woman who walked with a stick by each side. Her name was Martha and she sold soap made with nettles and beeswax. She'd mentioned the foxes. The colour of the place. Folksy things. She asked about the house.

'About time someone gave that place a seeing to. Kept the mould away.'

It was Martha who told him about the willow tree nearby. About the grieving mother living among the roots. People would leave children's toys at the base, baby carrots, small knitted things. But that was a long time ago, when the tree was still standing.

She asked about Pól, about Gráinne.

'It takes a village,' she would say. The crescent dip of her smile. Martha had been a midwife, "in another life," she put it. 'I'll drop over some soap for the mammy.'

Ben never meant to go looking for the tree. He had no reason to. It was long gone, after all.

He told himself the first time was an accident. But it was the same murmur he felt at night, the same weight, urging him forward in the naked daylight.

The familiar, twitching finger-ends of the branches beckon him on. Plantlet heads nod at him in the breeze. Whispers, kindling, dead songs, colour. Milk and blood. His mind goes.

And there's Martha, like always, smiling wide, head bent, rictus-mad, crooking slowly as he and Pól amble past. A midwife's watchfulness. Ben smiles back like they've known each other for years.

He carries Pól in his arms the rest of the way, climbs through a gap in the overgrowth, and the willow tree rears up before him. He sees the rummaging of grass at the roots. The long, spotted fingers. The torso rising from the dirt.

Ben held Pól to his chest the whole way home after his first visit. The shame was deep, angry. He was sick with it. He couldn't explain what he'd done, why he'd given his son over so easily. He'd never go back.

When it took Pól from his arms and went beneath the roots, he had to wait above ground. He wasn't permitted to follow, to think. Before long, he heard Pól's soft cooing again and there he was, content, reaching from the ground, waiting to be picked up. Only when they emerged from the birdless underbrush onto firmer ground did the haze lift and the world shift into place again.

Then, that first night back at home, the murmur in the dark was gone. They all slept. And Pól was fine. Better than fine.

It got easier after the second time.

It was always the same. He never knew what went on underneath. He would listen for anything earthly. If he strained hard enough to hear, there was something wet, distant, a suck and pump. But the dense haze on him made it impossible to focus, to parse.

At first it was once a week or so, then he stopped keeping track. He always knew when it was time to go. He could never recall the thing's appearance afterwards; the memory crumbled at the edges the more he focussed on it. A sallow meat thing. A face like wrinkled paper. Martha's voice in the air, sometimes, an old melody. The sound and the smell covered everything like rising damp.

After a while, the nights at home shifted in a different direction, and things were settling between Ben and Gráinne. A soft calm descended on the house. They slept well. They had sex for the first time in months. She held him again. She was his again.

He didn't notice the changes in Pól at first. He was paler, lighter. Gráinne noticed, of course, but the doctor found no reason for alarm. He was sleeping, he was feeding. It was good they were all sleeping.

'He seems happy', Gráinne would say. Did she know? It didn't feel like betrayal.

Every day it felt like the distance between them was mending.

It wasn't a price. It was a gift. A wonderful gift.

Ben arrives home and they spend the rest of their perfect spring day picking vegetables from the garden. Chopping, peeling, simmering. They make love. They drink time like nectar.

Pól sleeps and they don't yet notice the bright green of his eyes fading. The deep, slow rattle in him.

Ben rests his head against Gráinne's breast and she strokes his hair.

'The mould is clearing up,' says Ben. 'In the corners. Finally.'

'We still have to get the plasterers in,' says Gráinne. 'Always something.'

'Sure don't I look after us,' he says, and she flicks his ear. 'And aren't we doing fine.'

Pól wakes quietly and his fingers trace the branches outside the window and cling empty. He hears the patter of rain. He hears the squirm of roots and other living things sounding off in the night. Every call a belly-cry.

BLUEBERRIES

My boyfriend packed blueberries in the tote bag. I will discover this later when it is unsalvageable. I call him my boyfriend because we have been seeing each other for eight months. We haven't talked yet about if we are putting a label on it.

Boyfriend placed these blueberries at what is essentially the Mariana Trench of the tote bag. He was in charge of packing. I didn't ask him what he had decided was important for our beach day. If I had, he would have said that's micromanaging.

I always pack a blanket for the wind, and sunscreen for the UV, and sunglasses for the same thing, and a book for the boredom, and my headphones for the screaming children. I hoped these would be obvious things to boyfriend and he would pack them without me asking him to pack them. It's when he does things that I wouldn't do that the fights always start.

The tote bag is bumping along in the back seat of his beat-up Honda Civic, which doubles as the place where we eat our takeout, and he throws his laundry, and we have sex when his nosy roommate gets home early. He could have cleaned his car before putting the tote bag in it.

As it turns out, I took too long to get ready and now we are running behind the imaginary schedule that boyfriend made for us to follow on our day off. I'm late because my tits look great in this bikini and I thought maybe I would have boyfriend take pictures of me on the sand before I go swimming so I had to spend time on my makeup.

I tell him this.

I'm not complaining about the way your tits look, boyfriend says.

But he is complaining about being late and aren't all complaints about the same thing, in the end? It's the afternoon now and he's all: didn't you say yesterday you wanted to tan? I don't want to hear it if you're hungry when we get there. Straight to tanning. We're going to fry ourselves.

The air conditioning is warm at best, and it is sputtering at me at the same rate that boyfriend is. I reach over to turn the radio up and drown him out, but the seatbelt catches, and I am stuck in the spot. The fabric tugs against my bare shoulder. I undo the belt, so that I can turn the song up.

Will you put that back on?

Boyfriend is a stickler for safety. I was told that he gets it from his mom, by his dad, who hates his mom. I think it may be the fundamental difference between us, me whose mother died versus him, who learned it is okay to hate your mom.

I turn the radio on max volume and redo my seatbelt. Boyfriend is muttering a spell of curses under his breath now. I have half a mind to turn the radio back down and ask him to just say what he wants to say, but then I'd be giving him the reaction he wants.

I put my feet up on the dash. I take my time with it, admiring them as I cross my right ankle over the left. White nail polish is peeling off of my big toes and missing from the little ones. I'm not sure if they were ever painted in the first place, little stubs that they are.

The cops are out on the Parkway because it's the end of the month and they have quotas to meet. I see boyfriend glance at my propped-up feet every time we pass one. I'd like to see them try to pull us over for feet. The worst part is they would have to tell him the truth, about why they pulled him over, and that would be embarrassing for all of us. His car can only ever reach 60 mph, so they'd never get him on speeding. He's New Jersey's most hated driver, and we're perpetually in the right lane.

I'm barely listening to the music, but it is the loudest presence in the car. I wonder if I could go on like this forever, next to boyfriend, driving somewhere, not saying anything, mildly mad about something. Maybe this is love.

The shore begins to reel us in. I feel that I can taste the ice cream and the salt in the air. The ice cream, in particular, which we won't get on account of my being late. We cross the bridge from the bay to the boardwalk, Earth's own pearly gates. Boyfriend reaches over to turn the AC off and then rolls the windows down.

He doesn't bother with the radio. Here, you can play anything you want as loudly as you want. It's an announcement that you are alive. I look at the other cars, trying to play their music over ours. People are filled with the emptiness of summertime.

We are late, and the streets are aching from it. Vacationers and students home for the summer line the sidewalk. The cheap parking spots are full, tanning time is dwindling, and I'm longing for a lobster roll. But I can't mention any of it to boyfriend.

He drives around the crowded streets for fifteen minutes, circling the other cars like a vulture. I worry about what he would do if he saw an open spot.

He gives up his hunt after I beg him a few times and then he pulls into one of those $50 For The Day! parking lots that is closest to the beach. He will ask me to cover the cost tomorrow. When he turns the car off, we let the silence linger. My ears pulse where the radio beat for the last forty minutes.

Alright, grab the bag. I'll get the cooler.

I turn around to look at the bag I'm supposed to carry. It's not anything special, this tote bag. I forgot he had even packed a cooler. Probably mostly his beers. I get it now, why he was annoyed I was late. He thinks he did a lot more than me in the time it took to get my makeup on.

I slip my feet into my Birkenstocks and open the passenger-side door. From the back seat, I need to manoeuvre around some old blankets and a microwave he was supposed to bring to the dump three weeks ago. I pull the tote bag toward myself and sling it over my shoulder. No blanket, I notice right away.

Ready?

Boyfriend has pulled the cooler from the trunk. He locks the car and we start making our way to the boardwalk. From here, on the parched wood, we survey the beach like we're claiming land. I say that I see somewhere to the left, away from people but near the bathroom. I watch boyfriend glance to where I am pointing. He stares at it for as long as is reasonable before saying no.

Boyfriend has a thing against the left, I've noticed, which I think might have something to do with always driving in the right lane. We settle on the spot he picks out, pay for our beach passes, and then make our way to our territory.

Ah, forgot a blanket. He says it flat. Guess I'll just go for a swim then.

Boyfriend peels off his sweaty shirt and jogs away. He disappears amongst the mass of people who have descended upon the same place on the same day for the same escape from the same life, and eventually, I can't locate his head between all the other heads bobbing in the water.

I look around for the beach chair rentals, but then remember the $50 parking and think I better not. Instead, I dig a groove in the sun-scorched sand with my toes and sit down.

I peel open the tote bag like it's Christmas Day. He remembered the sunscreen and the sunglasses. I begin to apply some to my arms. Then I smell something vaguely familiar, close to rotting. I rummage back through the bag and my hands close around a hardcover book.

I pull out *The Glass Castle*, flipped upside down inside the bag. It was my mother's copy. Inside, she had written a list of all the pages she enjoyed the most. One of those habits that you tell people they don't need to do, but then when they die, you're so glad they've done it.

Now, her note is a smear of ink and blueberry guts. I panic and toss the book aside into the sand. I rummage furiously through the rest of the bag. It is just blueberries, in an opened Ziploc, oozing out. I scoop up the few intact berries and throw them into the cooler, where they should have been in the first place.

My eyes fall back on my mother's book, smeared by boyfriend's mistake. I want to be angry. I feel so angry I could throw up. I can't remember if I told boyfriend that the book used to be my mother's. I wonder if the boy who learned that it was okay to hate his mother would have packed blueberries in the tote bag, even if he had known.

His head emerges from the mass, seawater dripping down his soaked locks. He waves from the distance. I will have to speak with him, in a few dreadful seconds. I feel tears beginning to run down my cheeks. They are hot like the sun and salted like the ocean. They belong here.

ELLIE ALLAN

THE
WORM

You have asked me, begged me, spat at me words of such despair at my condition. My distance, my coldness, the brutality of my treatment towards you. Why I am reluctant to undress for you, why I turn to aggression and then withdrawal without a moment's notice, and for seemingly no reason. I suppose you must have speculated, concluding it must be a sore upon my soul. All the symptoms I display are that of a traumatised child, a personality disorder, some deep disturbance of my psyche. The truth is, my deepest secret is otherworldly. I fear you will not believe me, for my confession may appear to be a ridicule of your intelligence. I promise you, my love, everything I am about to disclose, despite the insanity of it, is completely truthful to the best of my knowledge. I ask for you not to question, nor doubt, for I do not understand myself.

I had just turned 12 and was staying at my grandmother's home in Dorset during the summer. The weather was sticky and the home had a terrible fly infestation. I ate canned peaches with a glass of milk every morning, followed by cucumber sandwiches and pork pies for each meal. It was not a terrible summer, but it was monotonous. There were children my age everywhere I turned, swimming in the rivers, running around and playing tag, but I was a withdrawn and awkward child. My earliest memories are not of actions or people, but rather a dreaded sense of shame and discomfort. I was often passed off to various family members and elderly folk as my mother worked in the petrol station just outside of the village. I spent most of my childhood in unfamiliar places, sitting silently on wooden chairs watching the news and drinking watered down juice and just waiting. I was always waiting for something, to be shuffled somewhere else. I had a deep and sincere distrust of men; I did not grow up with a father nor a brother and my grandmother gave me no uncles. My grandfather had died a year before my birth, and, like I said, I was raised by a series of elderly women.

At my grandmother's I had free rein of the house, garden and surrounding area, so I would walk and walk and find comfort talking to the neighbours' animals. Surrounding fields were filled with freshly-shaven sheep, chickens, cows and horses. There were only a few rules I was bound to follow. My grandmother was a highly superstitious woman, and my mother would frequently joke that she invented some of them herself. Throwing leftover salt over your left shoulder developed into storing it in a silver can until it was filled halfway, at which point it would be placed in boiling water and discarded in her tomato plants. She had established a series of complex rituals to prevent... what? I don't know. Her demands, as long as I stayed in her house, were to comply with her superstitions. I don't know whether her fear came from experience, rumours or paranoia, but this caution governed her daily life. Many of them related to the night, where the supernatural roamed freely. No bathing past 6pm, rosemary tea before bed to prevent sleep possession, and categorically no going outside once the sun went down. She had a brother, who died in undisclosed circumstances, and he'd suffered from such delusions in the extreme. My mother once confessed to me that her uncle had frequent and manic spiritual hallucinations that led him to believe he was an appointed messiah, the second coming and so on. He would handwrite manifestos, forcing them on unsuspecting by-passers and sticking them in public bathrooms. I don't suspect my grandmother believed him, but I imagine her interpretation of his condition has led to a great fear of demonic and evil forces.

I was pretty much a well-behaved child. I rarely went against what I was told, as it was not particularly within my character. However, one night at my grandmother's, I grew restless in my hard bed. That night did not cool the air in my room, and I felt the discomfort of heat deep within my bones. I could hear my grandmother snoring in the next room as I got up and peeped through the curtain. The sheep in the field below were illuminated like little silver beacons. I contemplated going down to them, I could do with moving. I was suffocating in this box room, and my mind wouldn't shut down; a walk would do me some good. I did not want to wake my grandmother, so I crept down each step. Despite the creaking of the Victorian staircase, she didn't stir. I took the key from on top of the fridge, turned it in the lock and slipped through the back door, skipping down the long garden, passing crab apple trees and her vegetable garden. I could barely see, for moonlight is not as efficient as a candle or a torch, but I had memorised the garden layout and intuitively made my way to the bottom. I could make out the fence that bordered the field, separating my grandmother's land from the farmer's. It was maybe twenty or so feet away from me, and I began to run towards the creatures, giddy and drunk on rebellion. In my haste to get there I lost sense of my surroundings, and must have been further to the right of the garden than I thought, near the shed where all the garden tools were kept. As I began to pick up speed, I tripped over an indistinguishable object and my body plummeted to the ground. This fall was nothing I had experienced in the past; I had been impaled by something and a hot, seething pain penetrated my stomach. I don't know how long it took me to crawl back to the house. It could have been 30 minutes, or 4 hours. I just remember throwing up three times and praying through gritted teeth.

When I made it home I laid on the kitchen floor to regain my breath, eventually crawling up the stairs and into my bed. Why would I not go and inform my grandmother of my ailment? I was far more fearful of my grandmother's anger than I was of my own pain. My sleep that night was filled with terrors as I fell in and out of consciousness. Giant winged creatures, reptiles and shadowy men filled my vision. Upon waking, the pain had completely subsided. Of course, I was relieved, believing my late-night antics were just some wicked dream induced by the heat. I lifted my top, which revealed, to my horror, a perfectly circular hole, the width of a two-pound coin, on the left side of my stomach. There was no blood; in fact, it seemed to be perfectly healed. The skin was soft to the touch, and it appeared perfectly natural. I pulled my top down and decided to think nothing more of it, no need to confess my sins and worry anyone. Maybe the hole would close up, since it did not hurt and was not infected. I continued the rest of my holiday as normal, in fact I actually felt pretty relaxed considering my situation. I had attempted to look into the hole while standing in the mirror, but it was impossible to discover how deep it went and I was far too squeamish to put my finger inside to find out. The inside, from what I could see, was pink, the same colour as my mother's hand after she burnt it on her hair straightener. After discovering this, I decided to place any thought of it in the back of my head, and I locked it up tightly in a cabinet of other troublesome memories.

While it sounds unbelievable, for a short while I didn't think too much about it. At that point it caused no change in my life, and I accepted my fate of keeping this secret to the day I died. It is funny what lengths people will go to conceal instead of asking for help, but it just did not seem like a possibility. I doubted any adult would know what to do about this predicament, and as I said it caused no problem at this time, and the hole was, well it just was there. The final two weeks at my grandmother's house passed, my mother came and we drove home. It wasn't until about a month later that I felt an intense cramp on my left side. Believing I had started my period, I ran to the bathroom but found no blood. It was the hole; I could feel it vibrating, at first subtly, and then with more vigour. A cracking sound, like when you open an egg over a bowl. My stomach hole began to gently tickle as I felt something wriggle inside, myself agape as I sat on the bathroom floor. And then a slimy worm head poked out. A worm had hatched inside of my stomach hole.

If I appear to be distant, and neutral when relaying this information please understand that is purely because of the passing of time. This happened when I was 12, since then I have had two decades of processing, replaying and eventually finding acceptance. In the following years, I grappled with the fact I now had a long-term resident in my body. What had impaled me that night? Was it something, or *someone*? Maybe a pitchfork, it seemed like the only utensil to cause such a wound. How did it heal so quickly? How did the worm egg get inside? Was it somehow catapulted into me while I withered on the ground? Was this the work of the devil, the demons and the spirit world? Was my grandmother right with her superstitions? Was this a punishment for revolting against my elders? It was most certainly supernatural in nature, that is undeniable. At times I considered this the work of my grandmother, as though she was the witch, holding out the apple and waiting until I eventually, and inevitably, succumbed to temptation.

Through the next seven years I learned to live with the worm. He wasn't particularly high maintenance, but I found myself craving abhorrent and rotten food; the desperate need for maggot-infested flesh and moulding tomatoes tortured my mind. I walked miles up and down tracks of the village, a heightened sense of smell directing to me to a week's dead bird or badgers. I ate them on the spot, shamelessly, until my appetite was satisfied. I went to the giant green bins behind the grocers and supermarkets, plummeting my hand into the mushy goo of decomposing vegetables, grabbing fistfuls of decaying sustenance and gobbling portions of putrid slop. The experience of relieving this craving has never more accurately been depicted than in Bernini's Ecstasy of St. Teresa, the Saint penetrated with an ineffable spiritual light. I imagine this is how I looked, plastered to the side of the wall in an unnatural satisfaction.

Those around me began to complain of a foul odour, and at school I was outcasted. My peers rumoured I had killed someone and from then onwards had been cursed to smelling like a dead body. Even the curious vampire group who drank each other's blood believed I was tainted by something they wished to stay far away from. My mother, who scarcely got closer than five feet to me, believed we had a constant sewage problem and was forever bleaching the bin and pouring concoctions down the sink. Over the course of a couple months, the smell began to subside; I suppose the bacteria in my gut became acclimated to what I was consuming. However, I remained in solitude. I had grown up with my own company and it prevailed throughout my teenage years.

Lying and avoiding became second nature to me; I conjured up an immense fear of water and thus was exempt from swimming on seaside holidays. I took no interest in crop tops and was hailed both strange by some, and admirable by others. Any unusual habits I picked up as a result, changing in the bathroom after PE and walking around with my arms wrapped around my stomach, were passed off as part of my odd personality and as such people mostly left me alone. I cared for the little worm for what reason exactly? I felt an obligation, as we had a shared, grotesque secret companionship.

I had the unwavering belief that I was to blame for this. I had been warned by my grandmother and ignored her instructions, and as a result I lived in concealment, fearful of investigation by others. I did not believe I was unique, but I felt like a cyclops cosplaying as a human. I had considered the possibility that other people also had a worm, or another creature, and settled my mind by vouching to make friends with anyone who disclosed their shared infestation. But no one ever did.

When I wasn't at school, I aimlessly walked from village to village, my head empty; I hated being inside, I would become restless and felt as though I were drowning. I was easily overwhelmed by internal architecture; I always felt like a fish stuck in a tiny tank and I would frequently throw up if I forced myself to remain indoors, or if the weather did not permit me to be outdoors. I, naturally, assume this was because of my worm; since we could not talk to each other, I never found out why he demanded this of my body. I was a hostage to a hostage.

Why did I never tell anyone? Well, simply because I was too fearful of what was to happen after I let this slip. Where would I begin? I feared being sent to a hospital, being tested on, being denied or accused of lying, and lastly, I just came to accept this fate. I did not want to expel the worm, and I was curious about what would happen in the future. I was fearful of the disgust of others, and equally fearful that, should I disclose this to another person, the worm would vanish alongside the hole, leaving me to be labelled mentally unstable. This is, after all, the most abnormal circumstance and I had no desire to draw attention to it. I also didn't know who I would even tell, my mother was so distant to me and I had no fellowship. I avoided doctors and never showed my midriff. The worm occasionally slithered part of his body out of the hole and allowed me to pet him.

My life followed with excessive dullness. I enjoyed very little but just drifted from place to place. I completed my GCSE's and then one year of A Levels before dropping out and going to a technical college because my grades were poor. I existed mostly in a nihilistic dream world; how could I possibly relate and connect to others when my life was being dictated by a squatting, possibly supernatural, invertebrate? I did not feel superior or special, I felt like an extra anomaly, on the fringe of the freaks and the creeps. You must understand, this was not a particularly eventful period of my life, it came and it happened and it passed and I woke up every morning and I walked and I attended my classes and sat watching TV or I walked about and occasionally picked feathers off the carcasses on the side of the road and this somehow filled my days.

During one summer, seven years after the egg first hatched, I slipped through the garden gate and walked through the empty pastures, passing small creeks and receiving momentary relief from the heat under large oak trees. Finding a resting place at the very bottom field before the border of the next village began, I smoked half a pack of Marlboro Reds, lay down and fell into a midday nap. I don't know how long I slept for; it couldn't have been more than a couple of hours, since the sun was still pretty high when I arose. In mild confusion, as is customary when exiting the dream world, I noticed my t-shirt had risen high and exposed my entire midriff. My worm was flat, burnt grey against my stomach. He had shrivelled, tormented by the sun as I slept on my side.

I picked him up by the head, and pulled him for the first time from the hole. His entire body had been dehydrated, he was dry and about twenty centimetres in length. I had killed him. I went to the nearest tree, removed some dirt from its roots, buried him, and began to make my way home. I checked my stomach a handful of times on my journey back, the hole still wide. I passed the stables and plucked a long hair from the mane of a chestnut mare. I reached home just after 6pm, and immediately walked to my mother's sewing box to pick out a small needle. In the bathroom I sat on the bathtub, threaded the horse's hair and stitched the hole. I did a sloppy job, but it was sealed tightly shut. I washed what used to be the opening with diluted Dettol and joined my mother for dinner.

I had no more problems other than the eye sore of the scar, which remained violent in appearance; my skin did not mend together and the horse's hair bobbled the flesh so that it rippled. I graduated college and got a job in an office, and have never spoken of this to anyone. I had never been pursued by anyone before, and so confessing to this was never needed. No one before had ever desired to be intimate with me in such a way past casual friendship. I have no desire to lie about this bizarre ailment on the left side of my stomach, but you must appreciate this is a difficult thing to lie about regardless; there is no possibility this can be explained by a surgery, botched or successful.

Two decades of complete isolation, due to such an impossibly far-fetched and unearthly situation has resulted in immense fear of discovery. I am unremarkable in every other sense but my worm made me one of the most peculiar accounts of human experience, and as such I have always felt as though I am in hiding. I am void of... what? I do not know exactly. I wake each morning believing I must have some mental disturbance, I must have suffered from hallucinations, a terrible fever causing such a nightmare. Yet I feel around and find my lumpy and bound flesh and reality once again dawns on me. How could I have accepted this so easily? Why was it I felt so unsafe in confiding in my mother, my grandmother? How could I, with all my facilities in check, continue my daily life with such welcoming of an infestation?

This is the reason, my love, that I have remained chaste, and prudish, and at times cold. I wish to experience joy, euphoria, drunkenness and love, and therefore you must know what I've held so close to my chest, protected and in a genuine amnesia, forgotten at times. The further I move away from the worm, the longer it has been outside of my body, the more I have felt discomfort in silence and seclusion. It is not enough to pray for a miracle, but I realise I must take some agency and cut ties with the worm and its legacy. Feeling so vastly different from others has been comforting and natural to me, a self-imposed prison put up to protect me from the insanity of my experiences and choices. When I lost my worm, I believed I could be an average, everyday person with no secret and maybe then I could experience love, and friendship, and every interpersonal connection I have missed out on. But this was really an optimistic fantasy, for when I lost the worm I did not lose my secret. When the worm died I still had this hole on the side of my stomach, an empty, hollow space. In sewing up the rim, I stopped anything else from filling that void. This is how I truly felt. And so, I remained alone and uncertain.

In our five years of knowing each other, you have gifted me with more small joys that you can possibly be aware of. Usually, when people look at me they squint ever so slightly. It's a peculiar habit of others. I notice them turn to me and almost immediately their bottom lash line raises ever so slightly. Not quite meeting the pupil, but closing the gap. The facial muscles adapt to this change of the eye, resulting in a subtle curling of the top lip, or sometimes a mild pout, and a raising of the eyebrows. The effect is quite unsettling once you notice it, a combination of both pity and distaste, also mistrust. But when you talked to me, during our first encounter, your face was relaxed. I spoke to you more only to test your reaction, waiting for your features to change. And yet they never did. It was your first day and as we would be spending almost eight hours next to each other, our friendship began out of necessity. Our bond grew through inside jokes, glances at Bill's eccentric shirt choices and Claire's relentless groaning about the HR department. Before long we were sharing book recommendations and our every day, absurd encounters at the Tesco Express on Market Road that always attracted an eclectic crowd.

I did not understand your advances for a long time; I didn't realise that your interest in me was genuine. This is why I questioned you so violently. Until you expressed to me that it was not merely my appearance or conversation that attracted you so strongly, but the small openings I offered you to see inside me – as though I were teasing you with breadcrumbs of my personality. That enraged me. I remember turning away from you in the computer chair, only for you to grab the arm and turn it back round, laughing under your breath.

'Don't swivel away from me, I don't mean it like that. I *meeean* I care about you. I want to see inside your brain and work out what it is that makes you, you, and what it is that is causing you so much trouble. I want you to let me in.'

The more time I spent with you, both at work and later in my fourth-floor apartment with Gino's takeaway, I began to feel that by your company alone, the void began to fill.

I wish to be close to you, for you have shown me the possibility of change, of love and of closeness. Still, sometimes I get anxious by your presence, and the desire to resort back to hibernation consumes me: you feel like an intruder, like my worm. This discomfort is a hurdle that I want to overcome. I have learned that there is a huge difference between wanting to want something, and actually wanting something. I have *wanted* to *want* to tell someone about my worm, and yet never done it because it is not something I actually wanted, until now. You have been so patient with me, but I know that even patience has a deadline. I hope you will not fear me, nor pity me or seek to heal me, but to accept the absurd and adore me for it.

MARISOL KARCS

STAGNATE

She came in the evening. The automatic light flickered in front of the garage. A dog barked – not mine. I was allergic to dogs. It was the kind of darkness outside that hinted that you should go home, to your home, and leave me alone. But my wife was on her shift at the nursing home, sticking IVs in prune skin and changing metal urine-soaked bedpans, and the chilli was still in the slow cooker, stewing, waiting for her when she came home. I had crawled into bed in my t-shirt, my slippers on the rug, and there was no dog beside me, because, again, I had none. There was a ring from the front door.

My life was nothing special, but I still didn't want to ruin it by opening the door for a stranger. I was just promoted to Near-Head Official in the office, one step below Head Official, the highest title on the thirty-sixth floor. I could tell that Brenda, the woman currently holding that title, was starting to falter. She would clutch her delicate gold necklace whenever she walked past my cubicle. This was because at one point I had joked that I would place a devil's curse on the poor woman if she didn't step down. Brenda couldn't sleep for five nights. These are the stakes in office jobs.

I was prepared to ignore the doorbell and fall back asleep when I remembered something my wife had told me just before leaving: That her aunt's best friend's friend would be travelling through the area and would need a place to stay.

'She might be coming in late from the airport,' Juliette told me. 'She's older, her name is Murphy. She used to be a mechanic. She has some weird habits.' Then she had caressed my cheek and placed a ghost of a kiss on my lips before grabbing the car keys from the bowl by the door and backing out of our driveway and into the wider world.

I loved my wife. Her hands were firm and decisive. Her cheeks were full of interesting anecdotes. She had a close trim, her chest was large, her belt was tight, and her nose was pierced. She smiled easily at strangers. She found me in a lesbian bar, on a first date with a different woman. She eyed my booth from the bar, sipping a beer. Her foot was tapping fast. Her lips were wet. My date was chewing on peanuts, and in between chews, she would say, 'That's why I think landscaping is the best job in the world,' or, 'My cat was hospitalised for eating my weed.' But all the while, my eyes kept slipping from my date's face, ever further until they passed the disco ball, the tables lit with candles, and finally the shelves of rum and whiskey. My now-wife's forehead was shining. She winked.

I enjoyed having guests over because seeing my home through their eyes reminded me that Juliette and I were happy and successful. Shortly after my promotion to the thirty-sixth floor, we had enough money to afford our first home: two stories, wood bannister on the stairs, five steps up to a small front porch, a balcony off the main bedroom, a newly remodelled kitchen. We were twenty minutes from the airport, a decision I made because listening to the sound of impending travel above us as we fucked put me on the precipice of excitement. Beside us, other townhomes. A park just down the street. Yes, we were part of a Homeowner's Association, and yes, we lived in a gated community. We had plans to start a family, but for now the extra bedroom was for guests.

Our life was good. Juliette was good. Something was wrong with me. These were new issues: for example, at the park, I sneezed uncontrollably, to the point of tears. It was only the park near our new townhouse that did this to me. In the grocery store down the street, the sight of Lysol spray bottles, all lined up in yellow perpetuity, would cause my eyes to itch. I don't think it was the colour; I don't think it was the latent cleaning chemicals wafting around the aisle. I think it was the promise it carried: of dutiful deep-cleanings, of messes and convenient fixes.

And then there were other things that I would rather not say, things that could not be easily explained. My skin was constantly buzzing, like rats crawling around the circumference of my head, my shoulders, the insides of my thighs. I was scratching my skin constantly. At work, when Brenda said something stupid, and I excused myself briefly from the meeting, I would stand in the stairwell and shake my head, scratch my elbow, sometimes kick my shoe against the wall.

One day during the morning meeting as I visited the stair-well, my eyes were drawn to the wall just above the floor; right where my shoe had met the wall countless times were tiny scuff marks. There were enough scuff marks to form letters from long vertical lines and shorter horizontal ones, which created a word against the concrete: FEAR. As far as messages go, it was neither subtle nor specific.

I shuffled to the door in my slippers. It was a weeknight, and my eyes were heavy from editing so many spreadsheets. Through the clouded windows, I saw a speck of whitish hair. The old woman, my wife's aunt's best friend's friend.

The air was cool on my cheeks as I swung open the door.

The old woman didn't seem so old, maybe in her mid-fif-ties, but still, she reminded me of the new wrinkles I was forming around my eyes. She looked almost six feet tall. She was thin. She was muscular. Her hair was boyish short, and not so much white as silvery blond. Her eyes were a harsh blue under the porch light. She had hard lines around her mouth and between her eyebrows. She had one backpack-er's bag, strapped tightly to her chest. Held loosely in her left hand was a limp fox.

'Welcome,' I said, eyeing the fox.

'This was in your driveway,' the woman said, lifting the dead thing to eye level. She held it by its plump tail.

'You can just leave it in the driveway, then.' The fox's tongue was hanging straight down.

'You can't waste what you hit,' she said, firm.

'I didn't hit it,' I protested.

It was rude to arrive on my doorstep in the dead of night and accuse me of killing a fox. However, the woman held the fox closer to my eyes, and with her other finger pointed to the fox's midsection, which bore the unmistakable mark of tire treads. I thought it must have been Juliette as she sped to work, too in a rush to notice the bump or the surprised squeal. But I didn't want to accuse my wife of such a terrible thing, and since this was a guest – a friend of my wife's aunt's best friend – I didn't want to offend this woman.

I stepped out of the threshold and invited her and the dead fox inside.

It was almost midnight, only halfway through Juliette's shift. I was embarrassed; ordinarily, I would have set the table, prepared a nice meal, and plumped up the pillows in the extra bedroom before a guest came. Juliette called me a thoughtful hostess, but ever since the strange sensations and the confusing stairway messages, my hosting skills were slipping.

In the dim light from the upstairs hallway, we took each other in. She wore a flannel button-up; she looked like a grizzled lumberjack. She didn't attempt to smile. Around her were tiny gnats, which had followed her in from the porch light. They crawled along the rim of one ear, they terrorised her eyes, but she didn't swat them away.

'I'm Fiona,' I ventured.

'Murphy.'

'This is my house.'

I expected her to look around, to admire her surroundings, but she just stared back at me.

'Uh, can I take your things? Do you want something to drink?'

'I'll take a tea.'

'Great,' I said, then walked towards the kitchen.

I was relieved to see that she didn't follow. I heard her in the living room, slumping against one of our three leather couches, plopping her bag beside her. The kitchen still smelled like lemon and bleach, from the Lysol I'd used on the counters just that evening. The slow cooker hummed in the corner of the kitchen, the orange light glowing. The moon lit the speckled granite counters, bounced off the steel refrigerator.

The faucet was leaking. Juliette had tried her best to fix it. My wife was a wonderful woman, but she was no miracle worker. She said that to the children of her patients. She'd say, 'I just take vitals and do what I can.' My wife had a voice that left no room for argument, which was what I liked best about her. She was dependable, and she had a lot of the answers, but even she couldn't help it if someone's old mom was chronically constipated, or if their dad refused to eat anything other than popsicles. And even she couldn't stop our faucet, six-hundred dollars of stainless steel with a pull-out function, from leaking precious water into the white ceramic sink. It was time to call a plumber. I didn't know when I had started to care about leaking faucets.

Murphy was still sitting on the couch by the time I emerged from the kitchen and into the dining room. The fox was laid out lengthwise on the mahogany table, its legs outstretched. It eyed me with its one visible eye. I stopped beside it; I'd forgotten about that. The fur was matted, the paws were black, and the tire marks were stark against its thick red coat.

'What do we do about this?' I asked.

Murphy didn't respond. I looked up from the fox and into the connected living room; she was leaning back on the couch, her legs spread, her hands on her stomach. Her eyes were closed.

'Murphy?'

I stepped into the living room, the mug of tea in my hand, the steam rushing upwards between me and my guest. I wondered if I should put the mug on the coffee table and nudge her knee. Or maybe take the tea for myself and sneak quietly back upstairs, to my still-warm bed. I thought of sleeping. I thought of the spreadsheets that needed my attention by eight o'clock tomorrow morning.

'Murphy,' I said, one last time. As I waited, I took the time to scrutinise her. The night was silent between these heavy walls; the only sound was her breathing. The bottom of her jeans were frayed. Her mouth was in a perpetual downturn, even in rest. Her hands looked dry. I hated the way her sweat mingled with my brand-new leather couch, then I hated that it bothered me. She looked lesbian. Her cheeks were coming close to the age of sagging.

'I don't believe in omens,' Murphy said. I jumped, the tea sloshing a bit. 'But killing a fox like that is definitely not a good sign.'

'Well, it wasn't me,' I said. I was tired of being chastised..

'Right in front of your house? That's bad.'

'It's just a fox.'

Murphy's eyes shot open. She turned to look at me. It was my turn to be scrutinised; she started around my eyes, my hair, then wandered to my feet. She returned to my eyes and simply stared.

I traded my weight between my feet, uncomfortable.

'What? I don't want it in my house.'

'Let me tell you a story,' she said. She turned her head to rest it against the couch cushions and closed her eyes again. 'I was working in the same shop all my life. I was the only woman there, but I was taller than any man I worked with, and stronger. It's because I knew how to lift with my legs. These guys, they went to the gym and worked out, biceps, triceps, whatever. They came in with these big muscles. They bent over and picked up tires like it was nothing – but they were using their backs. They always had to take an afternoon or two off every couple weeks, they were in so much pain all the time. They put ice packs on each other. They hated that the dyke never got hurt, that really pissed them off.

'This was the eighties, you wouldn't understand. You probably weren't even born yet. Anyway, one day this lady comes into the shop. She's broke, her car is shitty. I give her a quote for the car and she starts crying. She tells me she just lost her job. I dunno, I was looking at her pretty blond hair and I just said, don't worry, I'll cover it. She's so happy, she gives me this big hug, her tits touch my chest and I can't handle that these guys are watching so I push her off. I couldn't stand their eyes on her.

'She comes back the next week, after I finish fixing up her carburetor and replacing her spark plugs. I wouldn't let any of the guys touch her car. Not that they wanted to; it was my charity case, I was doing it for nothing. When she comes to pick it up, she says, "Wanna give it a test drive?" That's exactly how she says it. And I tell her I'm working. She says okay, I'll wait, and when I come back outside at five she's sitting on the hood of her car, reading a book.

'"Where do you wanna go?" I ask her.

'"I'll take you somewhere special," she says.

'So we drive away. The sun was setting; it was in the fall. She drives out of town but avoids the freeway. She stops by a corner store where everyone knows her, everyone smiles at her. She buys a six-pack of beer and we drive on. There start to be less and less houses. We talk about a lot of things, the conversation never dies. All the while she's driving me who-knows-where, I can't stop looking at her face, the side of her face. She had a really delicate face.

'Finally, she parks at the head of a trail.

'"It's getting dark," I say.

'"We're not going to walk far," she says.

'We walk on this trail that leads us through a forest of Monterey pines. The pine needles make it feel like we are walking on air. I started drinking in the car so I'm already a little tipsy. She grabs my arm as she's stepping over a dead log. Finally, in front of us the trees fall away and there's a cliff. There's nothing but ocean ahead, grey ocean. It's roaring, it's crashing onto this little hidden beach below us.

'We're standing side by side looking out. The air smells like salt, there are gulls below us squawking. Suddenly, I feel alive. I've just been working on cars all day, my hands still have grease in between the cracks in my skin, the back of my throat burns from all the exhaust I breathe in every day. I liked that air, though, that fresh wind on my neck that cooled off the sweat from walking, and the look of the sand down on the beach being destroyed, over and over. Beaten down and drenched.

'The girl looks at me sideways. Then she takes my hand and leads me down this skinny path to the beach.

'It was the most magical moment of my life. Her little pink smile. The way her hands moved. In the moonlight.'

Murphy stopped speaking. A silence emerged before she broke it.

'I quit the shop a little while later, and became a truck driver, because I wanted to see the country, and that's the cheapest way to travel, driving shit like fruits and cows around the country. Killed a lot of deer at night, those stupid fuckers don't move. I worked that job till my neck started to kill me. That's when I realised, sometimes the world gives you signs. Retired with a pension last year.'

She opened her eyes and looked at me. 'Am I boring you?'

'I have work tomorrow,' I said. It didn't matter what story she was telling, what past she was transported to. I was still in my world, and the off-ness of my life persisted, the slight wrongness I couldn't shake.

Murphy stood up, her hands on her thighs. 'It's a pretty fox. I'll deal with it.'

'Thank you,' I said, wondering what I was thanking her for; for solving the problem that she'd created?

I set the tea beside the dead fox.

'You live so pretty,' she said to my back as I wandered to the stairs, and whereas earlier I had been waiting for her to admire my home and my life, now I couldn't rouse any pride within me.

When I slept, I dreamed I was standing in swamp water. The water was still. The air was full of rotting frogs. When I turned around, I found the woman from Murphy's story, standing on a boardwalk, staring at me. She muttered, 'You must not waste,' and her gaze burrowed under my cheeks like worms. I also dreamed of barking dogs, except it wasn't a dream; the neighbour's dogs were barking, they always did when my wife came home. Juliette crawled into bed. Her skin was wonderful and warm.

I woke with a start. I suddenly remembered the fox, which right now would be leaking onto the mahogany. My family's table would be stained with fox and I would never get those dark spots out, not even by the time my children were born and were eating crackers off the table.

I ran downstairs, leaving my wife in bed. The sun filtered in through the frosted front door. My feet were barefoot. I stormed into the dining room, waiting to see that dark, dead eye, staring at the ceiling, staring at me. But all that was on the table was the mug of cold tea, the one from last night, and in it, several dead gnats, floating idly on the sunkissed surface.

I peered into the living room, but Murphy and her belongings were no longer on the couch. The guest room upstairs was also empty. Murphy must have left very early, but I didn't have much time to ponder; I grabbed a container of my chilli from the slow cooker and backed out of the driveway and onto the freeway.

Work on the thirty-sixth floor was tense these days. Brenda was eyeing me as I sat at my cubicle, her glass office directly across from my desk. I took lunch early in the break room, wanting to avoid my coworkers. That feeling from the dream, the worms under my cheeks, still nagged at me, and although I had checked my reflection several times in the mirror before leaving the house and felt around my face on the drive to the office, I still couldn't shake the feeling.

The overhead lights buzzed. I stood alone in the break room in the late morning, waiting for my chilli to heat in the microwave. I looked out the floor-to-ceiling windows on a cloudy day and squat brown buildings. Beside me were boxes of old files needing to be thrown out. The microwave kept spinning behind me. It was stuffy and airless in there.

Suddenly, a voice shouted from behind me.

'You'll never take my job! Never! Never!'

It was Brenda. She was clutching her necklace with one hand and gesticulating with the other. She seemed upset; I thought maybe it was the devil's curse from the other day.

The microwave dinged. I walked over to the kitchenette and retrieved my bowl. Meanwhile, Brenda followed me, still screaming. The steam wafted between us as I turned around to face her.

'Are you listening to me? I told HR what you did. You're out of here,' she said.

But I kept looking at my chilli. Something was wrong. The air smelled sour.

Suddenly, I was sweating. There was bile in my throat. And I couldn't say for certain, but between the beans and ground beef, the onions and the parsley, I thought I saw the delicate red hairs of the fox. I moved the spoon around and found a white canine.

My scalp was stinging. I could think only of Juliette. Right now, she was still in bed. The sun was lifting, and the light was grazing her face, first grasping her narrow chin, then stroking her forehead and visiting her short black hair. Her mouth, her chapped, rose lips, were flaky in the sunlight. But the sun didn't touch me here. The sun didn't touch me.

BRIÁ PURDY

THE
HAREBELL

From my spot on the hill I can still see the fishermen. They consolidate the slimness of light with their silent waiting. Great big chunks of sky leering down on them, staving off the inevitable. I take my notebook. I wonder what they see out there, standing in the horizon line?

I walk along the thin line of rocky grass. Bottlebrush grass in abundance and the sea daffodil continuous along three metres of the rocky face. I measure it; I write it down. The young green ash is stunted. I touch its rough stump and note its position on the cliff face. Plenty of rock polypody and woodfern. The fishermen stoop like herons across the horizon, but I am no longer interested in them. I burrow down beside the malnourished green ash, digging down to a small clump of ashy rock. Dead roots under my fingers. I take some pampas grass to smooth out the evening and wander back along the bluff.

When I first arrived on the island, they told me to find an uninhabited house and occupy it until it was time for me to come back. I chose this one because I liked its position on the bluff. It stuck out oddly and looked like it might at any moment grow limbs and a voice and proclaim itself a beacon or a landmark. Inside, there were lots of handmade furnishings and the kitchen cupboards were filled with tins. I spent a whole day categorising all of these possessions, noting down lace doilies, ten-piece china sets, dusty linen, furs hanging crudely in the wooden wardrobe. And, of course, the books. The small house was filled with books. Everywhere I looked, books stacked and crammed into empty spaces.

I suppose I liked the familiarity of the books and so I settled in the house on the edge of the bluff. I imagined myself becoming old within the paint-chipped walls, boxed in amongst the furs, letting myself curl into the springs in the mattress and never again seeing another living soul.

My days spill out around me and I order them like this: rising early to make my coffee and sitting awhile to read the previous occupant's books. Staring at my face in the hollow mirror and rubbing it until it is red and unfamiliar looking. Taking my notebook, pens, measuring tape and tools, and tucking them carefully into my rucksack. Venturing out into the world, my red mac slapping about in the wind and the rain, pulling the strings tight until my face becomes little more than a serrated circle. This small vantage point through which I glimpse a greying world. Then, I begin at the far end of the island, west of the little stone house. Or, I move down, surveying the beach, looking for washed-up seaweed and dead fish skeletons. No matter which way I go, I always come back to this: a wailing song, the sounds of wind through cracked palms, telling me something I cannot quite make out.

Reading by the dim light of the choking fire. This one edged in seafoam green, entitled *Near to the Wild Heart*. I chose it because it was on the bedside table, propped open, spine jutting out like dismembered hands from behind a rock. The previous occupant had obviously been in the middle of reading it. I pick up where they left off and settle into the faded armchair.

There is an order and a way to things that cannot be overlooked. I take great care to follow my routine, despite the growing hostility of the weather, the cold and dark that seeps like petroleum into the earth. There is no use in spontaneity. A purpose without function, without results. My methods are crafted in order to learn, to mark, to grow. I will soon discover that there are many ways you can write down the rate of death. There are many ways to plough through the bones of the deceased and not feel a thing.

A sapling withering away on the edge of the rocky path. It looks like how I remember a baby should be: wrinkled and precious, new-lipped skin and premature lines. Writing it down, I cannot help but remember. This suddenly becomes very painful. I squeeze my eyes shut and try to breathe in circles. I clench my chest and hear the scrunch of my raincoat. Raindrops drip onto my eyelashes. I count to one hundred and wait for my breathing to shallow out in pools. When I open my eyes, the memory resends. When I open my eyes, the rain has stopped falling.

I have known for a while that nothing will survive. It is clear that the island is inhabited by ghosts, or at least, soon to be ghosts. I cannot say if it is better or worse to know. To watch as everything around you turns to dust, mute as a bottle in the corner. To discover that it has already happened while you were sleeping, that while your eyes were closed and your breath was shallow, everything had already passed into that slippery and unreachable realm.

This morning, there is a dead fish at my door. A salmon, pink and perfect. I take it out of its plastic hiding and examine its slick flesh under the rain. There is no note, as usual. I take it inside and ponder how to make it last.

I make my way across the fields and into the village to post my letter the next morning. I take the long way so that I can feel like a martyr. I nod at the usual foliage as I pass, not wanting to stop, knowing I would want to stay a while and admire the curling flowers. Instead, I whisk myself away, climbing down the bluff and jumping like a snake onto the sand. My feet sink into the wet mass. I walk across like an astronaut, picking my feet up high and placing them down like I am planting a flag in an unmarked world.

The fishermen are out at last. The storm is passing and the clouds give way to milder bodies. Their unmoored boats float like rooted trees ahead of them. As I walk across the beach, I follow their blackened forms, still as anything, dotting the water like sitting seagulls. I wonder who is out there, what they are thinking.

The village green is empty because it is a bank holiday. All the villagers are off pretending to be pious. The children have scattered because they are afraid of God smiting them for disobeying their parents. Smashed glass frames an empty shop front. I post the letter through the postbox lips. I see Peter in the window of the post office. I smile and raise my arm, but he moves away from the window. I tighten my scarf around my neck, wrapping it all the way around my head, shielding my face from the rest of the world.

There is a boy playing with a deflated ball on the green. For a while, I watch, endeared, as he plays a pathetic, one-sided game of catch. The ball hits the wall unceremoniously and sinks to the concrete without a sound. The boy walks calmly to fetch it, returns to his spot and repeats the game.

I call across the green to him, but when he notices me watching him, he lunges for his ball and disappears down a side lane.

I continue walking.

I recall walking through my dreams, which were really, back then, canyon walls along the foothills of a place I had never been in my waking world. The sun was like the desert, harping down on me, as I walked from rocks to grassy mounds. I soaked in the day and wondered where I was going. It was all too easy to succumb to the monkey flowers and the penstemon, to lose myself in the small blue-grey rosettes that sounded like chimes. The sun moved across the sky, exposing the fertile ground. I noted the endemics that I crossed, not because I had to, but because I was a child and I was curious. My dreams were often like this; in the ones in which I was a child, wandering alone, free to press the sharp cactus arms too close to my face and smell their musky alloyed scent, their spiked kisses were feather-light. I knew they would not harm me. Only when I wake do I find myself surrounded by a cruel and bitter silence. Does it really count, I ask the peeling walls, if no one is here to give me good wishes, to wish me health, to prop me up against the doorframe and mark how much I've grown, to sit me down on the pile of undone washing and stranger's books to ask me what I imagined I might be when I grew up, who I hoped to become?

There is a storm in the night. When I wake up, the sky is bruised and dripping. I make a coffee and potter about, trying not to think about my dream. There are fruit flies batting about, fighting over the forgotten plums. It is not the season. They are anomalies, just like me. I flick the puckered skin and watch the flies rise for a moment, dispersing like currents. I stare at the fruit, rotting away in the fruit bowl. They look like an old, withered face. A face with skin like leather, sun-worn and soft. Two foul plums, one sour grinning face. I put on my boots to go out to work. The fruit flies decide it is safe to return.

Sometimes, when I was a girl, I tried to talk to God. I could hear my father shutting a door and retreating into an unreachable keyhole. I could see my mother keeping watch at the window. She knelt and prayed. I knelt, too, a tiny mollusc at her hip, and rallied against my mother's prayers with secret wishes of my own. I squeezed my eyes shut and laid my head on my mother's cold arm, praying the only way I knew how. By the candlelight, our kneeling forms made shadow puppets.

The first time I took the ferry across that impossible sea I knew I would not return. My mother and father became like spectors haunting the past recesses of my mind, folding back into drawers, becoming lost items I might find occasionally and bring back out into the light, only to realise they no longer belonged to this new and frightening world. I folded them up neatly, carefully. I put them away, along with all childish things, and set about making my new life in Dead City.

Dead City had another name, though no one used it anymore. I worked in a laboratory with pristine curves and glass walls. I forgot there was ever such a thing as home. Dead City was certainly no one's home. Cruelty went by entirely unremarked upon. On the underground, in the streets, in the middle of the day. There was poverty and desolation and dirt. Everyone who was left seemed to me to be miserable or alone. Ambulances blowing their sirens all hours of the night, wailing from invisible mouths, foxes fucking in the dark alleys and homeless kids rummaging through empty bins for old batteries and bits of uneaten meat. It was like stepping into a new order full of violence and noise.

The University was like a mirage, presenting a grand plan in the wake of this widespread despair. Inside its wrought-iron gates, we did not fight or scream at one another; in fact, we did not speak at all. Each focused on their own task, their own small part of the puzzle. It was a lonely and woeful place. Most days I saw no one, spoke only to the broken vending machine on the third floor corridor facing the stairwell.

I became accustomed to the silence during my days spent crouching over specimens in the laboratory. Only when I left the gated perimeters of the University building, did I enter once more the wall of unadulterated sound. Despite the brutality, the unwavering stream of violent sounds, I was grateful to feel like I was entering a world which was alive and fighting to stay so.

Sometimes when I close my eyes in the silence I still hear the sounds of Dead City. Cars crashing into grilled metal fences. Glass smashed and faces turned inside out. Abandoned bodies played with by bored orphaned children. Animals out all hours, hawking, howling, fucking anything that moved against the backdrop of red stained brick. Hairless old women thumbing loudly through mouldy stacks of outdated fashion magazines under the streetlamp by the park. Sons screaming down disconnected landlines that might as well be a void. Everything collecting, collating into one, steaming, all consuming sound.

Even in such a desolate place, an island separated by the wide open ocean, I remember the sounds because it is not so easy to forget. Perhaps I do not want to forget. Because even in the horrific sounds, there is a voice. It clings onto my memories of Dead City and pleads with me beyond the crying window frame. His voice, my voice, the soft sound of our footsteps. In the midst of such chaos, such awful resurrected sounds, I can still hear his words, coming to me across the sea and rocking me gently into the night.

I met him by accident. Coming out of the blinding white snow, dressed like an eskimo. I saw him immediately and watched him make his way carefully across the glistening tarmac. It was nothing, really. A shift in the light, suddenly unbearable, which reminded me of something long abandoned. A kindness, a mistaken kinship. He stopped and saw me. He raised his hand as if he knew me. I noticed the patterns falling into the sludgy ground. Surprised, I waved back. This small act breached the distance between our stupid, raised hands. I laughed for the first time in weeks. At his figure, our hands, still waving across the empty parking.

In Dead City, time passed inconsistently. I spent my days testing for bacteria. I spent my nights walking along the highline park, counting the variations of fern leering over the edge of the abandoned railway lines. Often he joined me on these long, inebriated walks. We said very little, though sometimes I grew brave and asked him to tell me about his work. He was a physicist and worked at the University, too. I was fascinated by the way he would take his own hand and explain to me in abstract and confusing terms the strange dance of the smallest particles. I liked walking by his side and listening as he confessed his resentment towards the University for making him stay here, in Dead City, when there were other places out there that he could go and conduct his work. *Other places,* I thought, the phrase jamming oddly against the metal railings as we reached the end of the promenade. We were not in the habit of making jokes. We said goodbye clumsily and then he turned and hurried off into the dusty night.

I wake in the night to the sounds of thrashing winds and collapsing air. Explosions, loud and sharp. Intervals of silence and then cheers of mutiny. Behind the soiled curtain, flashes of light. I close my eyes and burrow back down into the bed. Under here, there is darkness and the promise of safety. Under here, I can close my eyes once more and return to that impossible highline, where together we walked into Dead City.

Armeria, agapanthus, kelp and juniper. Dwindling, folding over, drying up like old maidens in the uncaring of a new day. My microscope remembers them all. I measure them out of respect; I cover the dead in the rusty earth. Plough over and through. Dead bird. Dead spider. Dead ants on the mound. I tick off the bodies in order of size. I note the position of the sun, watching behind the curtain of dark clouds. Down by the marsh, I find a collection of firecrackers, piled like bones by the base of the severed black willow. The sounds that had woken me: fireworks, deadened and dull in the remains of the day. I dispose of them neatly, careful to roll them first in dampened soil and then string them along like fish on a line in the cold, dirty water. Christened like infants, I put them in my rucksack. Back at the house, I will lay them out in the bathroom to dry and then place them on the mantelpiece along with my other adopted treasures.

Hamamelis virginiana. Witch hazel. One of my favourites. Its toothed ridges look sharp, but they are as soft as can be. Pubescent like an alien, covered in white hairs. I examine it carefully, kneeling down into the ground. Its flowers are premature, budding despite the unripe stem and lowly position. I turn them over carefully in my hand. On the underbelly I can see the beginning of sickly, yellow spots. The disease has set in. There is nothing to be done. The structure will open. The flowers will wilt and die. The stem will harden and turn black. I stare for a while at the poor thing, remembering all over again. It will have to be carried to term. It will produce nothing but dead seeds. It will be forced to go through the motions of life when all around there is no hope of survival.

Perhaps once I had believed there was a chance for a different ending. Perhaps when I walked with him across that skyline and we talked into the violet night. Now, I am no longer sure. Now that I know what it is to be shelled like a clam, rid of my most precious thing, I am alone to wonder what is there left worth saving? I realise that I am just like the witch hazel: forced to carry this dead weight, the burden of my failed experiment, until the very end. But when it is over, when I have purged myself of all hope, what am I supposed to do with what is left of me? When I am over and empty and a fruitless throbbing womb, what am I to do with the body, the thing that carries, this pointless, ugly husk?

He told me, on the highline, safe from prying ears and distrusting eyes, that he was afraid of the future but that he did not believe it was hopeless. I wanted to touch his face and see what it was that he saw. Around us, every night, the domesticated growls of a churning machine held us accountable for all that we said and all that we longed to say. He told me he had always imagined himself with a family and conceded that after everything, after all, he was a conventional man at heart. The apophthegm, *tomorrow is another day,* he repeated often and with a wry smile. He knew that now it was impossible, and that made him long for it even more.

Jazz on the radio. I am washing the dishes in the kitchen sink while leaning towards the window, trying to catch the last of the golden light on my face. I feel myself opening up like a flower. The broadcaster announces that Szabó Gábor has died this evening in Budapest, from health complications. I listen absent-mindedly, thinking about another place, far from anywhere. *San Francisco Nights* plays through the house. I have never been to San Francisco. I imagine the sun is different there. I remember a line from one of the previous occupant's books I had just finished reading. It confronts me from across the foamy water. There is a heavy aching in my belly. I place my warm hands onto my chest and leave them there until my shirt is wet through. *When I was alive, I aimed to be a student not of longing but of light.*

So much can be glimpsed about a life from the things that occupied it. The books, for example. I am making my way slowly through them. Some are worn, pawed-over, creased, the signs of a well-used copy. Others are pristine, untouched. I wonder if they have ever been read. I wonder if I am the first to touch their uncracked spines and delve into the worlds there waiting.

What became of the previous owner of this house, I cannot say. All I know is that we have the same taste for hand painted pottery and wear roughly the same size clothes. My favourite: a blue silk nightgown, trimmed in lace and as slick as the still morning sea.

He told me his favourite colour was blue. Not blue like the summer sky or like a bottomless ocean, but blue like the colour of the streets in the pueblo where he grew up. Fractured and scraped, solidified in his child's mind as the bluest of blues. That was his first and favourite colour.

My eyes are also blue. He smiled and told me not to close them until he was gone.

There are no fishermen this morning. They are perturbed by the weather, the growing whip of the tide, pulling itself close to the cliffs, smashing its liquid body against the rocky face. Today the sky is a mirror. Glasslike and grey, almost white. If it could speak I am sure it would sound like a child, mimicking language it has heard but does not yet understand. I have brought my magnifying glass. I want to identify the ridges and marks on broken seashells. I spend the morning categorising their details. I make a sketch or two in the bottom corner of the page, and then, pleased with my rendering, turn to a full page and copy it out in large.

Sounds coming from every waking thing. I turn my head, the waves rising, running, breaking, fizzing and then fading at my feet. The beach is empty. The sky is greying, pregnant with overdue clouds that seem heavy and impatient for a change of circumstance. How did we all find ourselves here? I think about how everything is dying or already dead, and grow woeful. I clench my fists and lift my head into those abounding clouds. For the first time, I grow doubtful. Why am I here? What is the point, what does it matter anymore? Why had I been sent here to watch everything disappear?

I climb up Bray Head to escape the claustrophobia of my own company. I remember the way in the dark, in the rain, the snow. It is steep and it takes me longer than usual to reach the top. For once I am blind to the leafy tracks. It does not matter to me anymore that the glossy, arrow-shaped leaves have a name that I should remember. There is no sense in recalling such a useless epithet, only to come back, later, much later, to find that it, like the others, has died.

Instead, I walk with my eyes sealed shut. My mouth like a creaking door as I puff and pant my way along the steep decline. From this vantage point, the whole island lies spread out like a compass or a map. Lines leading one way and then another. Spotted trails connecting every little part to something significant.

From up here, I can see the beach, the ridge of the cliff and my little house. It looks dark and uninhabitable. It seems fitting that a ghost should occupy such a place. But could it be true that have I become that see-through spectre, seeing out the days, just waiting for time to cave in on itself?

I cannot sleep. In my mind I am back in Dead City, sitting at my laboratory stool, watching through the myopic lens of my magnifier. Infinite structures reveal themselves. Hatching lines making walls and rooms and great open fireplaces.

In the half-darkness, I feel around inside myself until there is light. I imagine I am that young boy's deflated ball, being filled up, brought back to life. Someone is looking after me, playing with me religiously. Silence stretches around me in that small room, but I fill it with my loneliness, pressing deeper, more frantic, wanting to scream and wake anyone who is left.

He is here.

'A miracle,' he is whispering, pulling me into his lap.

When he is gone I go to the bathroom to stare at myself in the mirror. I touch my hot skin to be sure that I am real.

I touch myself and cry out to the stone walls. The horror of my own pointless body sobers me slightly and I stop myself, quivering all alone and burning with something like love. I lick my traitor's hand and it tastes like metal.

Afterwards, I fall asleep instantly and do not stir until morning.

There is nothing new for me to report. All the sea lavender is brown and crackles beneath my feet. In my hands it crumbles to nothing. To dust. I count how many are missing or lost. The wind howls but will not tell me where they have gone. It is depressing to write it all down, but I do it. I seal the report in the white envelope and write the familiar address on the front.

Out on my usual rounds. Skipping over the dead roots and upturned heads, the wreckage of the previous storm. I note everything carefully, like always. For a moment I am simply an observer, watching, collecting, settling down amongst the numbers and decimal points. Then, coming to the end of the bluff, I look down to the beach below.

A dead sheep on the rocks. But beyond that, something else. A small clump of perfect blue petals, hanging over the edge. The pause hangs, trembling, and I try to understand it. For the first time, I can feel his breath on the back of my neck, a phantom hand at the base of my stomach. I step back, shocked. The flower is real and perfect below my gaze. Pulling up my hood against the onslaught of wind, I run back along the ridge, laughing like a witch in the mud-slicked rain.

That evening, I pour through my books and try to identify those blue petals. I find it eventually and spend a while reading about its specific characteristics against the dying firelight. *The harebell blooms in the height of summer, its delicate flowers cannot withstand the harsh conditions of winter.* I wonder how it survives. I cannot quite believe it. That night, I dream in shades of blue, his words whipping around me and becoming a flower. You are there, too. For the first time in a long time, I can bear to peer into your face. A perfect, budding secret finally given form.

C.T. O'MAHONY

FRUIT OF THE EARTH

The garden had many secrets. Things buried. Things forgotten... And it moved. *Moved.* This wasn't a case of branches swaying in the wind or things getting blown about; this was bushes uprooting themselves and running across the lawn. It all had something to do with the gear house – a small, inconspicuous structure that leaned against the back of the cottage. It was made from old red brick and had a roof of rusted sheet iron. Father said it predated anything else on the property, although that hardly seemed possible, since the cottage was *old.* Three hundred years old, at least.

Father operated the machinery inside the gear house day in, day out. When his back started giving him trouble, he enlisted the help of his eldest daughter, Nuala. Then she went off to college and became bookwormish, which is to say disinclined towards manual labour. So the task fell to the middle child, Orla, who was more eager to please anyhow. Evlin, the youngest, had only been inside the gear house once, back when she was just a toddler. Whatever she'd gotten up to had left her with a jagged scar down one cheek, and a lifetime ban, which was fine by her. It left more time to explore the garden.

She liked to venture as deep into it as she could, and then find a good hiding spot. The gorse bush was one of her favourites. Its needles pierced her skin in places, but it was the last place anyone would look for her. Also, it smelled pleasantly like coconut.

Evlin had never seen a coconut, just the desiccated variety her mother dusted on cakes. How her mother liked cakes! Fairy cakes, fruit scones, swiss rolls, gateaux... She'd pile them on trays in great toppling stacks. They filled countertops, end tables, bookshelves, nightstands... there was even a tray resting on the toilet cistern. These were never eaten, and quickly began to rot. Then again, the house was full of rotting things. So was the garden, but the scent from the gorse bush hid a great deal.

Evlin had been hiding under it for hours. Long enough for the garden to grow tired of sitting still. The roots beneath her started to flex, and then the bush was off. Evlin clung on as best she could, only coming out once the roots had re-planted themselves.

She found herself in a kind of topiary. The smallest sculpture portrayed a snail. The largest, a bear. She greeted the latter as she walked past, but she didn't dare pet it on the head. She found a pile of discarded garden ornaments just beyond the topiary. It mostly consisted of faded Santas and snowmen, but there were several gnomes in there too, and even the remnants of a manger. The pile sat at the entrance to a hedge maze. Evlin lost her bearings almost as soon as she stepped inside, but it didn't really matter. Even if she'd memorised her route, the garden would have kept moving – kept changing. It was always best to forge ahead.

Eventually, she came to a hawthorn tree with rags tied to its branches. Some were neat ribbons of expensive looking fabric; others were rough squares of hessian that looked like they might have been cut from a potato sack. Evlin tore a swatch from her own skirt and added it to the collection. It was a gaudy pink and orange material that clashed with everything else in her wardrobe, but it blended perfectly here.

A robin landed on a nearby branch, tilted its head, and blinked at Evlin. Then it fluttered to the ground, pecking at something in the dirt. Not a worm or an insect – it was too big for that and looked like it was made of blue plastic.

'Fruit of the earth!' Evlin cried, and started to dig it out with her bare hands. She was hoping to find a bottle cap. She'd collected several already, but didn't have *quite* enough for a necklace. This wasn't a bottle cap, though, it was an old car battery. Father had probably lost it at some point. The garden had a way of disappearing things, only to return them later on. Sometimes weeks later, sometimes years.

Evlin repacked the earth over the car battery, lay herself flat on the ground, and whispered: 'Swapsies.' Then she jumped as someone cried: 'Scarface!'

It was Orla, calling her in for dinner.

Mother would have given them cake for dinner if father had allowed it. Instead, she cooked savoury dishes with the word "cake" in the name. Yesterday, they had crab cakes. Today, pancakes. The batter was thick and claggy.

'Eat!' mother said, shoving a second plate towards Evlin.

'Yes, eat,' father said, despite the fact that he hadn't so much as touched his plate. He was too preoccupied with his newspaper. Nuala was just as bad. She had brought an entire stack of books to the table, as though she might work her way through them all by the end of the meal. Only Orla actually ate. She ate quite a lot, but never got fat.

'I saw a bear in the garden,' Evlin said eventually as she poked her pancakes with a fork.

'You didn't see a *bear*,' Orla chided. 'You're such a liar!'

'I am not!' Evlin cried.

Orla rolled her eyes. 'Tell her, Nuala.'

'There haven't been bears in these parts for two and a half thousand years,' Nuala said without looking up.

'See?' Orla asked.

'It wasn't *that* kind of a bear,' Evlin said in a small, whiney voice.

'Your face looks so ugly when you scrunch it up like that,' Orla said. '*Extra* ugly, I mean.'

Evlin threw a pancake at her, but it went careening over her head, and landed atop some mouldering fruit scones mother had made several days earlier.

'Now, now girls,' father said, turning his newspaper. There were piles of those about the place, too. In between all of the piles of rotting food.

'Eat!' mother said again.

Evlin stuffed a forkful of pancake into her mouth and huffed unhappily.

It was days before she found the hawthorn tree again. This time it leaned over a koi pond, with no hedge maze in sight. She dug between its roots where the car battery had been, and unearthed a one-legged Barbie. It had matted auburn hair and a purple tutu.

'Oh, thank you, thank you, thank you!' she squealed, and rushed back to the house to show her sisters. She found Nuala sitting cross-legged in a fort made from stacks of books. Nuala refused to so much as peek her head out to see the Barbie, and Orla was still in the gear house with father. Evlin would have to make do with mother. She found her in the kitchen, surrounded by dirty dishes. The cabinets were splattered with batter, and the floor had floury footprints all over it.

Evlin ran over and waved the Barbie about. 'Look, mother. Look, look, look!'

Mother looked, albeit briefly. She had a mixing bowl under one arm, and a wooden spoon in the other. 'That's nice, dear. Be a darling and pass me the–'

Evlin ran out onto the patio before her mother could finish the sentence, and hid between the raised beds father had built. One contained an overgrowth of rhubarb; the rest were empty, save for some rotting mulch.

Mother tut-tutted. 'You're getting too big to play all day!' she called out from the kitchen. 'Someday soon *you'll* be the one making dinners, you may as well get a little practice.'

Evlin didn't go back inside until she heard Orla and father coming out of the gear house. Nuala was still in her book fort. Mother was serving colcannon cakes. These seemed to be another variation of fried potato, but with an even thicker, gloopier consistency than the pancakes they'd had the day before. There were also some stringy green vegetables mixed through. Evlin wondered if they were from the raised beds, and moved her plate to one side.

'You'll never guess what I found today,' she said, and placed the Barbie on the table. Father didn't look up from his paper. Nuala didn't look up from her book. Only Orla looked, but she didn't seem that impressed.

'You'll never guess what *I* found today,' she said.

It was a ring. A *silver* ring, with a purple amethyst and tiny marcasite crystals. It was tarnished, and left a grimy mark on Orla's finger. Still, it trumped Barbie.

'I found it in the gear house,' Orla said, and held her hand out for Evlin to admire.

'Father should decide which of us gets to keep it,' Evlin said sheepishly.

Orla scowled and snatched her hand back. 'No way, Scarface! I found it, it's mine!'

'Now, now, girls,' father said.

Mother pushed Evlin's plate back in front of her and commanded her to eat.

Orla would not be persuaded to part with the ring. Not in exchange for one-legged Barbie. Not in exchange for *anything*. Evlin had even offered to pull a shift for her in the gear house.

'Don't be stupid, you're not even allowed *in* there,' Orla had sneered.

Evlin thought that if she could get inside, she might be able to find her own piece of jewellery. A necklace, maybe. A real one, made of metal, not bottle caps.

She petitioned father, but he wouldn't allow it – not after whatever had happened the last time.

Weeks went by before Evlin found the hawthorn tree again. This time, there was no koi pond, just a series of boulders and an old, rusted washing machine that had tipped onto its side.

The robin was back. It sat atop the washing machine, head tilted to one side.

'You can take your stupid Barbie back!' Evlin said, flinging the doll to the ground. 'I want a ring, like my sister's! Or I want her to lose hers. If I can't have a ring, she shouldn't be allowed to have one either!'

The robin blinked, and then fluttered away as Evlin started digging a shallow hole between the roots of the tree. She placed the Barbie inside, covered it over with earth, and whispered: 'Swapsies!'

The next time Evlin came upon the tree, she dug several holes around its base, but they were all empty. Meanwhile, Orla had found not one, but *two* new pieces of jewellery in the gear house. The first was a plastic hair clip in the shape of a sea-shell. The second was a threadbare friendship bracelet. She wouldn't even let Evlin touch them, let alone *wear* them.

'It isn't fair!' Evlin complained over dinner.

Orla stuck out her tongue.

'Now, now,' father said. 'Your sister's been working hard in the gear house, Evlin. Perhaps if you help mother tomorrow in the kitchen, you'll find a piece of jewellery of your own.'

Evlin's jaw dropped, and Orla snickered.

Mother placed another corn cake on Evlin's plate and commanded her to eat.

Evlin had no intention of working in the kitchen. She was getting into the gear house, with or without her father's permission. This proved to be easier than she had thought. The gear house was locked with a large padlock, but the wood of the door itself was spongy and rotten. Evlin kicked a large hole in it, and crawled through while everyone else was sleeping.

The first thing that hit her was the heat. The second thing was the smell, which was metallic and suffocating. She pulled the wool of her dressing gown up over her nose as she scrambled to her feet and made her way over to the machines. Contraptions might have been a better word for them. They were an amalgamation of burning furnaces and moving parts:

pullies pulling, wheels turning, cogs whirring. They seemed to go on forever, even though the gear house was no bigger than the average garden shed – on the outside, at least.

Evlin found all sorts of treasure: train sets, bowling pins, toy soldiers... but they all seemed to be a part of the machinery, and so she was afraid to touch them. Finally, just when she was beginning to lose hope, she saw something glinting in the darkness. An earring, maybe. She had to balance on a pipe to make her way over to it. The metal felt gritty and hot under her bare feet. She was about halfway across when she felt it give. The whole thing snapped in two, sending her sprawling head over heels. She let out a groan as she hit the ground and then the room began to fill with burning steam. The machines started to whirr louder and louder. The pullies started to screech. Soon there was a great bang, and then another. Evlin tried to crawl back the way she'd come, but the door had moved, or perhaps it was everything else that had moved... she wasn't sure.

She started to cry. Finally, a hand grabbed her shoulder, and she was bundled over someone's back.

Father.

He dumped her out on the patio and ran back inside the gear house.

Orla stood over her in a dressing gown. 'What did you *do*?' she asked.

'There's no time for that,' mother snapped. 'Go help your father!'

Orla stomped off unhappily, and mother pulled Evlin to her feet.

'Don't worry, dear, everything's fine.'

'Everything's *not* fine,' Nuala said, staring out into the garden.

It was... *churning*. Great clumps of earth were being flung up into the air, only to crash back down with a great spray of dirt. Evlin could see cogs and wheels in the mix, as well as the washing machine, the gorse bush, the little snail shrub... It took hours for father to get it back under control.

Orla lost a finger assisting him – the one with the ring. Apparently, it had gotten caught in one of the machines as she tried to undo whatever Evlin had set in motion.

'I only meant for her to *lose* the ring! Not for it to be ripped from her, finger and all,' Evlin told a carp several days later. It was no longer in the koi pond. They hadn't been able to *find* the koi pond, just some of the fish, flopping about on the lawn. Evlin had rescued as many as she could and put them in a plastic paddling pool with a cactus pattern on the side.

She hadn't been able to find the hawthorn tree. Partially because she'd been trying to avoid Orla, who spent most of her time in the garden "recuperating." Recuperating and digging. She'd found the one-legged Barbie, drawn a scar down one of its cheeks, and hung it by the neck over the dining room table. No one said anything about it while they ate. Nor did they say anything the next day, when it appeared that Orla had cut off one of its fingers. The day after that she severed the arm entirely at the elbow. The day after *that* she cut off its one leg. Eventually, only the head remained, dangling by Barbie's hair.

Evlin hid under the gorse bush when she could find it. Other times, she climbed into the trees. It was maybe a month before she came across the hawthorn tree at last, nestled between a dilapidated green house and a large clump of Angelica. The little robin was there, pecking between the roots.

'Fruit of the earth!' Evlin cried, and started to dig. She sucked in a breath when she spotted something purple in the soil.

The amethyst ring.

Evlin dug around it, and sure enough, there was her sister's finger. The blood was still wet and gloopy, as though it had been severed only yesterday.

Evlin wondered if they might be able to sew it back on.

'Scarface!' Orla called suddenly. '*Dinner!*'

Evlin paused, and then placed the finger back in the hole. She covered it over with soil, brought her face low to the ground, and whispered: 'Swapsies.'

LYNDSEY CROAL

TRIPHYOPHYLLUM SANGUIS

I inherited the *Triphyophyllum sanguis* from my father, his mother before him, and her father before her. Dad once said that my great-grandfather grew it from seed, keeping it healthy, fed, rooted, and hidden for decades. Now the plant appears older than time, thick stems dappled and grotesque. Climbing vines stretch outwards from its centre, with hooked leaves that seek to take over every inch of the space it inhabits. Every month I carefully coil the vines around the base, so they don't become unruly. It would be a soothing practice, to tame the plant's wild nature, if not for the rotten scent that oozes from it, cloying at my throat, until I feel like it's coiling around my neck instead.

The *Triphyophyllum sanguis* is different from other plants in that it doesn't require light – it gets its glucose in other ways. It was once small enough that I could keep it potted and out of sight in a kitchen cabinet, but now it takes up an entire box room in our house, locked so only I can enter. It used to be Noah's photography studio, but I needed the space once Iona became older, curious, and more prone to looting or climbing cabinets.

'Mummy just needs the room for herself,' Noah explained to Iona once, after ten straight minutes of "but whys", when I told her she couldn't look inside.

'Is it dark there?' Iona asked, trying to peer around me.

'Looks that way to me,' Noah said.

'Are there monsters?'

'Hmm.' Noah crouched down, whispering to Iona, 'Best not stick around too long to find out.' Then he scooped her up, and screaming and giggling together, they ran off. Now whenever Iona passes the dark room, she has the same response, turning the avoidance of the door into a little game – running away from Mummy's secret monster.

I hope she loses interest in the room eventually, even though she'll likely inherit the plant, or a cutting of it, when she's older – then she'll be glad I kept her in the dark.

I've learned over the years that I can't go far from the plant for too long without tiring or feeling on edge, so I have to make sure I plan my days around it. If I don't tend to it, I feel its hunger acutely. On the worst days, tremors take over my body until I return to the plant and feed it. It can't live without me, and neither can I without it. A symbiosis, of sorts.

Noah thinks the daily ritual has become a burden, but he's never really understood its needs, the hold it has on us, on our family. Before the plant became too wayward, he tried to put rules around it, which at least gave him a sense of control for a while. For instance, when we went on holidays, he insisted on getting it a separate room, so it didn't become disruptive to our plans; on those trips I would still sneak out and sleep in the plant's room, especially on nights when it was particularly hungry and needed extra care. Noah never said anything about it, whether he noticed my absence or not.

Now the plant has grown too big to take anywhere with us, so I stay at home most of the time, even when Noah goes away with Iona to his parents or for weekend breaks without me. Those times usually coincide with periods when the plant is especially hungry – when its leaves have begun to darken, as though blighted by some uncontrollable disease. I have to stay by its side, in the dark, for hours, until it's sated. After a while, it settles, my own exhaustion passes, and Noah and Iona return home. I keep tending to the plant in secret, regularly feed it and coil its vines carefully, and for a time, we're a big happy family again, pretending that the dark room houses nothing but knick-knacks and old boxes.

'Have you tried replanting it outside, to test if it can grow without you?' my therapist suggests during our weekly session. She's become very interested in the plant since I mentioned it in passing. Noah was the one to ask me to start going to these appointments, but now I'm regretting it.

'It needs me,' I say, knowing she won't understand.

'How so?' she asks.

I don't tell her the truth because she'd be disgusted by it. Noah doesn't even know, though perhaps he suspects, that every morning, I go to its room and let the vines wrap around my wrist, hook into it, and feed. 'If I don't look after it, it will die,' I tell her.

'Would that be such a bad thing?' she says. 'Letting it go.'

'Yes.'

'Why?'

'Because I can't survive without it, either.'

The plant's been taking more from me lately. I've become sluggish, distracted. My doctor referred me for tests as they're concerned about blood count. I've lost weight too, but some days after a feed, I lose my appetite, like it's fed me too, and all I can manage is water.

I'm visiting Mum when she notices the dark circles under my eyes. 'It's the plant, isn't it?' she asks.

'No.' A lie she sees right through because she's been here before. Dad died of heart failure, caused by acute anaemia. But that won't happen to me because I'll get this under control. I've got a system, a balance.

'How did you do it?' I ask, to change the subject away from me. 'How did you let the plant live here?'

She avoids my gaze, looking out the window, a distant look in her eyes. 'I had no choice, really,' she says. 'No matter how much I tried to get him to give it up, to let it wilt and die, it pained him too much to be parted from it. And I loved your Dad. I had to accept the plant would always be a part of his life.'

'Why did you let him give it to me?'

'Sweetheart.' She sighs, looking back at me, tears in her eyes. 'You were already so attached to it. I just... I thought maybe you'd manage it better than he did.'

I look down and scratch my wrist, rubbing the needle-sized spots where the hooked leaves have made their mark. I see Mum notice it too, unblinking in her gaze.

I want to stay here longer, to be with her, but I can feel the growing call of the plant, pulling me home. It's hungry. If I don't go back soon, we'll both suffer for it.

As I leave, Mum squeezes my hand. 'Just don't give it to Iona,' she says, her expression hard. 'Don't make the same mistakes we did.'

I arrive home just as the tremors begin. Noah calls through from the kitchen, asks when I'll be ready for dinner, but I don't answer. Instead, I head straight for the dark room.

The corridor lights are on, and there's giggling as I approach – Iona, chattering away, like she's playing make believe. I round the corridor and freeze. Iona is sat in front of the dark room door, holding up two of her dolls towards the base, talking in a high-pitched voice to the foliage that, to my horror, has started to creep out. Tiny tendrils of leaves, crawling across the floor.

'We're going on an adventure,' she tells the dolls. 'To fight the monsters!' She bounces them forwards and the leaves move closer to her, attempting first to dig into the plastic flesh of the doll, before moving on, dangerously close to Iona's hands. I rush forwards, and push her away, out of reach of the leaves.

'Don't touch it!' I shout at her. 'I told you not to play here. You need to stay away.'

Iona falls back awkwardly, drops her dolls in front of her. She looks up at me with wide green eyes, a look of confusion passing across her gentle face, not understanding what she's done wrong. Then she starts to cry, a wail that pierces through my already throbbing head. I look to the door where the leaves have now retracted into the dark, then back to my daughter, a seed of guilt now blooming in my gut.

I let out a breath. 'Sweetheart,' I lean down for her, intending at first to scoop her up, but I move away when I realise my hands are shaking. 'I'm sorry,' I say. 'Mummy didn't mean to.'

Noah appears in the corridor, drawn by Iona's wailing. He looks between us, then at the door. The look he gives me is sharp and cold, disappointment rooted in his expression. 'What happened?'

'She shouldn't be playing here,' I say.

He leans down and picks Iona up, cuddles her in close. She sucks her thumb and digs her head into the crook of his neck, still sniffling away. 'Shh, now, it's okay,' he reassures her.

'I saw the monster,' she mumbles. 'We were going to fight it, but Mummy came, and it ran away.'

Noah gives me another look, then he marches out the room. I make to follow him, but he shakes his head. 'We're going to do some stories before dinner,' he says in a tone that makes it clear I'm not invited. 'Sort *this* out,' he adds under his breath. 'It's grown out of control.' He throws a final glance back to the dark room, then heads upstairs to Iona's bedroom. A moment later, her nursery rhymes are playing, and then she's jumping up and down around the room, singing along, *'There was an old lady who swallowed a fly…'.*

I turn my focus to the door and open it with trembling hands. The plant seems to pulse as I walk closer, leaves and vines stretching and unfurling. It's grown too big, I realise, too unwieldy and I've been too exhausted to notice. Noah is right. I close my eyes and take a deep breath. I'll not feed it tonight. Starving it for a few days will do it good, stem its growth. Instead, I coil the vines around its base, tidy it up so there's no risk of it stretching out of the room again as Iona passes by. After, I stand looking at it, vines twisted unevenly. There's a ringing in my ears, and I reach out to it, as though my hand is being drawn there of its own accord. But just as the hooked leaves reach out, I snap my hand away. 'Not to-night,' I tell it, the image of Iona's crying face in my mind. Before it can tempt me again, I rush out and slam the door.

Once Iona has settled down, we have dinner. Noah talks away to Iona, but he ignores me. I sit in silence, pushing the pasta around on my plate, taking small bites here and there. The whole time, all I can think about is the plant, how hungry it must be, a sharp pain rising from my wrist, up my arms, to my shoulders, like invisible hooks have latched onto every part of my skin. I grip my hands together under the table, staring out the kitchen door towards the corridor.

'Elise, did you hear me?' Noah says, pulling me out of a reverie.

I look up to him. He's attempting to wipe Iona's mouth, covered in tomato sauce from the spaghetti, but she's doing her best to fight him off amidst giggles.

'Sorry,' I say. 'Did you ask me something?'

His jaw tenses. 'Will you be okay to pick Iona up tomorrow?' he asks. 'I've got a work meeting I can't miss.'

I blink at him. 'Yes, sure. Of course.'

'Promise me?'

'Noah, I think I can manage to pick up my daughter from school.'

He nods. 'Okay then, thanks,' he says, then looks me in the eye. 'And I was thinking, maybe you could start looking for a job again. It would be good for you to get out of the house a bit.'

'I can't,' I say, looking to the corridor. 'I've got too much to do here.'

'Iona's in nursery now,' he continues. 'And things are getting tight.'

'But...' I can't go out, I need to be home, to look after the plant. 'I'll start looking,' I say, if only to delay the fight. I look behind him again, an overwhelming urge seizing me to stand up and leave the two of them, to go to the dark room, but Noah gets up first, starts to clear away the dishes. When I look down at my hands, I find my nails have dug into the skin, small droplets of blood visible on my wrists. I wipe them off and get up to help Noah with the tidying. He looks to me as I stand by him, a hint of a smile on his lips.

'You can do this,' he says, as he squeezes my shoulder. 'One day at a time, okay?'

Noah takes Iona to school the next morning. As I busy myself with the household tasks, I find I'm making excuses to walk past the dark room again and again, as though to reassure myself it's still there. No tendrils have snuck underneath the door this morning, and though I hover by it each time I pass, I resist the urge to open it.

One day at a time.

Noah has left a list for groceries, so I head out in the afternoon. My hands shake as I hold the paper, my head in a muddle as I take my time gathering each item. With every few steps along the aisle, it feels like I'm moving too far away from home, too far from the plant. Its hunger is ravenous now, and a pain stirs in my gut, acidic and sharp. I clutch my side but continue along, determined not to let Noah down again, even as dotted lights dance in my vision. As soon as I've paid, I head back to the car, turn on the ignition, and clutch the wheel so tight my knuckles turn white. As I drive to the exit, instead of heading right to Iona's school, I find myself taking a left, towards home.

I wake up in the dark room. Vines have twisted around my arms and legs, the leaves hooked in deep, warm blood trickling across the bare skin. My mind lurches, a haze of confusion. I feel like I might be sick.

How long have I been here? I remember being at the supermarket, driving to get Iona... but the rest is vague, as though something took over my body.

There's a knock on the door.

'Elise, are you in there?'

'Noah?' My voice is hoarse.

'I'm coming in.'

'Iona... is she...'

'She's at my parents'. The school called when you weren't there for pick-up.'

'Oh.' The guilt of it stretches over me, digs in deep, as the door opens and light floods in. 'I'm sorry.' I shield my eyes. 'I don't know what happened.'

Noah takes in the sight of me with an expression I hardly recognise – repulsion, anger, pity? His eyes land on the plant, and he sucks in a sharp breath. 'I'm taking you away from here.'

'No,' I say. 'Please, I can't go.'

He ignores me and starts peeling the plant away, making quick work of it.

There's a tightening in my chest, a pain like I've never felt before. 'Stop,' I plead. 'You're hurting it. You're hurting me.'

'Your hands are cold,' he says, his words frantic, still tearing at the plant. 'You've lost too much blood.'

'It needs more,' I say distantly. 'It always needs more.'

I reach out for the *Triphyophyllum sanguis* just as Noah carries me away. A vine rips from it, trails from my clenched fist. As I glance back at the dark room, the rest of the plant oozing, wilting, dying, I can feel the leaves of the broken vine pulsing, desperately trying to take root in my veins. Logic tells me to just drop it now, put an end to it all. But even as my vision fades, my hand grips it tight. Without me, the plant will die. And I without it.

Will I not?

BRYAN MILLER

TO THE GOD OF TEETH

I spent my final night of fatherhood alone, in the barn, checking over the Jeep one last time, using a pair of rusty pliers to yank out molars that had grown in the carburetor and a row of bicuspids along the engine block that threatened to chew into the fan belt. It was a simple job made tedious by the incisors on the tips of my fingers that make my hands clumsy. I'd work all night if I had to. I'd just think about my daughter, Georgia, and her perfect thirty-two, and whisper a little prayer to the God of Teeth.

I'm not a religious man. Most of us aren't, which would probably surprise outsiders. Enough time has passed that people must assume our lack of internet and electricity is a pious sacrifice, as opposed to government prohibition. Folks forget their history so fast, even the history they've lived. We haven't had any new books in the library for almost 35 years now, but

I've read most of the old ones still there, and that seems to be the overall theme. Fiction and non-fiction alike.

Once I was confident the Jeep was in fine working order, ready for its one and probably only voyage, I cleaned up with a wet rag and some lye soap and walked back to the house. First I double-checked the padlock on the barn door to keep my secret safe, mostly for my own piece of mind. Is it even a secret if nobody cares what you're hiding?

Georgia sat at the kitchen table, working on one of her drawings. She was so wrapped up in her creation that she didn't hear me come in. I stood over her shoulder and studied the way her hand seemed to float over the paper like a cloud, leaving behind intricate lines in fine carbon grey. Her long blonde hair was pulled into a ponytail, a style she never wore outside of the house. She preferred to keep her hair down to hide the coffee-brown birthmark that ran across her cheek and circled around her left eye. I must have told her a million times how silly it was to hide a face so beautiful on account of one little dark splotch, but kids are sensitive.

The drawing in front of her depicted an elaborate castle constructed around an enormous waterfall. It looked like something out of a fairy tale, except the lines and dimensions of the structure were perfectly precise, an architectural marvel located in an imaginary fairyland.

'The only way that place could be prettier is if you lived there,' I said.

Georgia startled out of her reverie, flashing me that perfectly limited smile. I reached out and gave one of her shoulders a light squeeze.

'Jenny, I wish you could see this,' I said to my wife, who sat in her rocking chair in the living room. 'Georgia's designing us a brand-new house.'

Through the doorway, I could see Jenny nod. She couldn't look at the picture, or at Georgia either. She hadn't seen anything since the teeth had grown into her eyes years ago. I know it pained her to have never seen our daughter as a teenager or a young woman. Sometimes when I told Jenny how lovely Georgia had become, my wife's eyes chattered with jealousy.

Georgia said she was ready to turn in for the night. She packed her pencils into the antique silver-lined makeup kit with the opaline signet on the top. Her mother gave it to her for Christmas years ago, since she had long stopped wearing makeup. The makeup case became her art-supply kit. She carried it with her everywhere. Georgia kissed my cheek, said goodnight to her mother, and padded upstairs to her bedroom. I walked Jenny into the bathroom to get her ready for bed. After she used the toilet, I brushed the teeth in her mouth, then the ones in her eyes, and rinsed them out with splashes of water from a plastic cup. As I wiped her cheeks dry I described Georgia's drawing to her, even if I couldn't quite capture it with my words. She was smiling when I helped her over to the bed to lay down for the evening.

I stripped down to my underwear and got under the covers next to her. The sound of her snoring started up just a few minutes later. I was wide awake, though. It wasn't just the ache from the cluster of wisdom teeth calcified around the base of my spine, painfully ridged just beneath the skin. I wouldn't sleep all night, thinking about what I had to do the next morning.

I rose as the first rays of sunlight bent around the curvature of the Earth and drew a dark blue line across the horizon. I slipped back into the clothes I'd worn the day before to avoid the creaking of dresser drawers or closet doors that might wake Jenny. Then I walked as softly as I could up the stairs to Georgia's bedroom.

The walls were papered with her drawings. I could make out the shapes of them in the dimness, but not the colours of the lavish castles and towering trees and mystical beasts of her own creation. She lay sleeping on her side, curled into the foetal position, a spray of blonde hair across the pillow. My daughter, my only creation.

I gave her a gentle shake and whispered her name. She stirred, blinked at me. I put my finger to my lips. I told her not to wake her mother, that we needed to go somewhere. Her eyes were still bleary when she came downstairs to find me waiting by the kitchen table. I nodded towards the door. She followed me outside.

'Where are all the rest of my clothes, are they in the wash?' she asked when we were on the porch. I shushed her again. Jenny liked to sleep with the window open to feel the breeze, and I didn't want my wife waking up to our voices outside as we headed to the barn.

I opened the padlock and swung the barn doors wide. The Jeep was waiting there for us, blue tarp laying next to it like a shed skin. I couldn't shake the feeling that something would go wrong, now that I was so close. I told her to get into the passenger seat. She rolled her eyes.

'Daddy, what are we doing out here? It's not even five in the morning.'

I fished the key out of my pocket and slipped it into the ignition. The Jeep started right up.

Georgia gasped. She'd been in a working automobile before, but not often. Most of the cars in town had fallen into disrepair, and nobody had much use for them anyway, since there was nowhere to go.

'Oh my gosh! How did you do that?'

I couldn't help but smirk. It's a strange comfort for a parent to know they can still surprise their kids.

'Your old man's still got a few tricks, eh? Buckle your seatbelt.'

I backed the Jeep out of the barn and let it roll at idling speed into the dooryard, down the driveway, onto the empty road. The path I'd planned out would take us all the way through downtown, or what used to be downtown. That was out of pure necessity since the bridge heading in the other direction had collapsed long ago. A couple times I'd heard folks say the government had blown it up, which wasn't exactly true. They had barricaded it during the initial quarantine, but that's all. Like most things in this town, it'd just shrivelled from neglect. One section had collapsed when the river swelled up over the banks twenty years ago and nobody had bothered to replace it. But there was no explosion, just the slow degradation of time.

'This is so cool!' Georgia said. She held her right arm out the window to feel the wind slipping between her fingers. 'Where are we going?'

I kept driving. I'd forgotten how pleasant it was to lay down the accelerator and feel the road speeding beneath you.

I asked her, 'Do you remember what I told you when you were little, about how the town came to be this way?'

She shrugged. 'Kind of. You said the rest of the world didn't understand the magic of this place, so they left it all to us.'

She parroted my lie so easily. It was unsettling to hear such a bright, curious person repeat the line of BS they'd been fed. But then I'm the one who fed it to her, and she trusted me. There were hardly any kids in town anymore – not very many adults still around, for that matter – and they'd never grown up knowing life could be any different. As far as they were concerned, this town was pretty much the whole world.

'You ever hear anybody say anything different?'

She paused for a long moment before she responded.

'Blake Saxton said the land around here got radiated or something, so it's not safe for people who didn't grow up here. And that's what causes the teeth. Margaret Ellis' mother told her we were cursed by god.'

Poor Margaret Ellis. That girl's frown wrapped nearly around her whole head. She must have had sixty or seventy teeth just in her mouth alone. Her mother had been married to the last preacher we had in town, before he hanged himself with a length of fence wire.

'What do you think?'

She turned away from me to look out the window at the countryside blurring past.

'I guess I don't think about it much?'

'You don't, huh?'

She stayed quiet. She couldn't deceive me as easily as I could her. That made my belly go hot with shame.

'I'm not so sure anyone around here remembers, not really. People in this town have a funny way of forgetting things when they really want to forget.'

So I told her.

The town had been isolated to begin with. That was just the nature of living on the western side of North Dakota, where there's really no good reason to go unless you found a little oil well or could frak it out of the deep tar sands. You might have called it the middle of nowhere, except that it wasn't the middle of anything.

If we were cut off back then, it was by our own choosing. I'd only been away from home for a few nights here and there, to go to Bismark, and once on a four-day trip to the Wisconsin Dells. At its peak, our population was a smidge over 600, before everything changed.

We know the name of the boy responsible. Derek Olson. I played basketball with his younger brother, Chris. Derek was a senior in high school at the time, and a handsome kid, a speedy runner in the relay and on the cross-country team.

Derek was speeding down Reservoir Road one evening. Drunk, or maybe not, it doesn't really matter. Too fast, too careless, maybe too boozy. Either way, he ran over the Carrington girl, Genevieve. Seven years old, going on eight. Just about the sweetest little girl anyone had seen around these parts. She won Junior Miss Apple Festival, sold Girl Scout cookies out front of the Aldi, collected coins for the March of Dimes.

After he ran her down, Derek Olson panicked. He must have seen his whole future going away. He figured he had to make her disappear. Take the body out to some remote spot – goodness knows we have plenty of them – and give her an amateur cremation, then bury the ashes. But he also knew that police could identify a body, even a burned one, by the dental records. So before he stuffed her in the trunk of his car he cleared all the teeth out of her head with a tire iron. While he drove away he flung them out the window by the handful into the weeds along the shoulder of the road, like a bloody-handed Johnny Appleseed.

Genevive's disappearance was all anybody could talk about until two weeks later, when the first plants started growing along the side of Reservoir Road. Strange flowers, like dahlias, but with teeth stuck in the centre where the stamen should be. Folks started digging them out of the ground and potting them.

It all happened pretty fast after that. People started finding teeth inside of acorn shells, inside of the green apples growing on trees in their front yards. A farmer who raised corn for cattle feed shucked one of those ears to find that the whole cob was just one big grin inside.

Midwesterns don't like to draw much attention to themselves as it is, and a lot of people were ashamed by the strangeness of it. People only talked about it in whispers, amongst themselves, and not too many were keen to share it with outsiders.

Somebody did, though, because some inspectors from the Environmental Protection Agency and the Department of Agriculture showed up. They wound up summoning several dentists from the East Coast who filled up the motel and spent a few weeks wandering around, picking flowers and plucking fruit to search for hidden teeth.

The situation changed when Roberta Krimpasky gave birth to a baby boy that came into the world with a full set of chompers. Not little baby teeth either, big ones. I heard he couldn't even close his mouth. The doctors pulled all of them out, but within a few more days they grew back in. That poor child didn't live two months. Right around the same time, Everett Lee, one of what passed for our town councilman, died of sudden cardiac failure. When the coroner from the next county over opened him up looking for the culprit, he found Everett's heart full of molars.

Turns out, several people around town had found new teeth growing in, crowding their mouths, scraping their throats. They'd tried to remedy it themselves, ripping them out with pliers and bleeding in secret. It wasn't just their mouths either. They could feel the new teeth raising lumps under their skin, biting into their bones.

When the government people caught wind of that, they issued a quarantine. They kept it quiet, which wasn't too hard. Just blocked the bridge on one side of town and the highway on the other side, and the lake to the north took care of the rest. Just a minor re-routing of traffic. Who would even notice?

The teeth kept growing. Little flashes of enamel peeking out from underneath a strip of tree bark. Premolars and in-cisors pushing their way out of just about anywhere – the crown moulding of peoples living rooms, in the spokes of bike wheels, spirals of them climbing up the telephone poles, biting into skin from the armrests of rocking chairs. The whole town was teething.

The government cut the phone lines and blocked the cell towers. The power didn't go out for a few more years. The bridge stayed blocked, the roads barricaded. And we were all stuck here.

It's amazing, really, what you can get accustomed to.

The expression on Georgia's face was as clear and sharp as the lines in her drawings. The narrowing of her eyes, the way those green irises darted back and forth when she was pro-cessing new information. The slight pinch of her lips when she was holding something back. I always could read my daughter like one of those old library books.

'This isn't all entirely new to you, I'm guessing?' I said.

'I heard of Derek Olson before. That you weren't supposed to say his name or something. That his ghost lives in a well.'

I couldn't help but chuckle at that.

'I don't know about ghosts. Derek is down in a well, though, behind the Parker house. About a year after he ran down Genevive Carrington he got drunk and let something slip about it. Some of the local men questioned him. I think we still might have had a sheriff at that point. Either way, he told them what he'd done, and they did what they did, and now he's in the well.'

Just then, we passed by Jim and Annie McCord's place. Annie couldn't walk anymore with what her feet had become, but Jim still grew a little patch of crops like me. We helped each other around harvest time. He also had one of the last children left in town, and the youngest, a boy they named Silas. Jim and his son stood slack-jawed on the lawn, staring at the working automobile rolling past. The boy's whole face was pocked with teeth like white acne. I waved out the window.

'Off to the races!' Jim shouted as we blew past them. He snatched off his hat and shook it like a racing flag.

The boy's face made me grateful and ashamed at the same time. When Georgia had been born with that birthmark, just a harmless dark patch of skin, we hadn't thought anything of it. That she'd been born without any extra teeth haunting her tiny body was gift enough. Part of the reason there aren't many children around town anymore is they don't often survive childbirth, or much longer afterwards.

Georgia was self-conscious about that birthmark even before she could talk. She'd tug her hair down over it or turn her face away when anyone came to the door. And I guess some of the other kids might have been a little mean about it, which only got more ridiculous as they started blossoming orthodonture in strange places while my girl never had any but the old-fashioned number of teeth, all of them between her nose and her chin, straight as a newly-built fence. As she got older we even told her, if people ask, just say the rest of your teeth don't show.

I slowed the Jeep as we passed through the two blocks that used to constitute downtown. None of the stores were open anymore, not even the bar. People used to congregate there still, more out of habit than necessity. I'd take Georgia into town to socialise with the other kids and maybe for me to have a tipple of sour mash with Charlie Ford, who brewed it up and was always happy to have a drinking buddy.

The windows of the stores were all black now. The paint had chipped, the wood had faded. With no one bothering to pluck them, the walls and support beams were ridged with teeth in clusters and strands, canines hanging from the gutters like tiny icicles.

And on the big sloping hill behind the old general store, right near the apex, a bright gleam of enamel where a molar the side of a boxcar pressed halfway out of the ground, the grass still growing on one side of it while the exposed half was as wide and flat as an altar.

'Daddy,' Georgia asked again, 'why won't you tell me where we're going?'

We came to the part of the trip I'd been dreading the most. Second-most, anyway.

Half a mile past downtown, the road curved toward the Depot and the roadblock. The Depot served as the supply station to the whole town during the first years of the quarantine.

It was a squat, grey warehouse the government people had built up in a hurry. A green Army helicopter would fly in dangling a massive pallet with all manner of aid: dry goods, canned vegetables, MREs, soap, cans of gasoline, toiletries. And lots of toothpaste, of course. For a few years a couple of Army boys in biohazard suits would be in charge of dispensing everything. Eventually they just started air-dropping the pallets and left us to our own devices, which was no problem since the population had dwindled to near nothing. No reason to fight, there was plenty for everyone. One day, the choppers stopped coming altogether, for what reason I do not know. By that point the very few of us left were used to growing our own food and picking the teeth out of it. The Depot was still partly stocked to this day. I know because that's where I got the gas two months ago, when the motor of the Jeep was still only halfway rebuilt.

And a mile past that, the roadblocks. Massive concrete barriers six feet high, extending well past the shoulders of the road on either side, where the hills plunged into ravines that flooded during the spring and fall.

I felt Georgia's hand tighten around my wrist as we approached.

'This is why I had to look for a Jeep,' I said, and swerved off the road.

Georgia screamed.

I just had to laugh. Probably it was all the tension of waiting and planning finally bursting like a blister, and the feeling of the tires skidding beneath me, the plunge of the vehicle as I steered it towards the dry part of the ravine that had filled in and flattened with time.

The Jeep's tires steadied as we eased in the shallow part of the ravine. Then the cab tilted backwards and sideways as I steered us up the opposite slope and cranked the wheel to turn us parallel to the road, so that the steepest part yawned open beneath the driver's side of the vehicle. Beyond that, the road, and the great stone barricades as we zipped past them, past the edge of town.

Georgia braced herself against the window and the dashboard, knuckles white, her feet jammed down into the floorboard. But she'd started laughing too as we jostled and jounced along the rain-rutted ground. The Jeep threatened to tip sideways more than once, but after another half mile I found what I'd been hoping for – the one thing I couldn't plan out – another little shallow patch in the ravine that let me steer back onto the road.

Just like that, we were on a state highway. I saw no other cars on the road. I jammed down the accelerator.

Georgia hooted 'This is amazing!' out the window as her blonde hair whipped behind her, her face tilted towards the sun.

She started asking me so many questions that I didn't have a chance to answer them, which was a blessing. I took a few turns, navigating by the rising sun and heading northeast as best I could. A few miles later, I saw a rust-dusted road sign that said a town called Belleville was 14 miles away. I vaguely recalled the name.

'It's been so long, I don't know what's become of the world outside of town,' I told her. 'I don't know if the government stopped dropping off supplies because they forgot about us or because nobody cared anymore or because they couldn't. I don't know what folks are like anymore, or what they want or what they get up to. Although I expect what they want never changes much.'

I kept my eyes on the road but I could feel Georgia staring at me. I knew her curious smile was fading.

'I wish I could tell you more, give you some advice. But I can't. All I can tell you is to be smart and be careful. Use your good sense. It'll all seem strange at first, but if you can just tough it out, get your feet settled, you'll be surprised how you get acclimated. I know you will.'

Georgia asked what I was talking about as we passed the sign for the Belleville city limits. Not much of a city, although with a population of near 8,000 it might as well be. We came upon a cluster of businesses, a motel and a gas station and a McDonald's with glowing yellow arches. Those I did remember. I slowed the Jeep and turned into the parking lot, in one of the farthest spaces from the motel.

'I've got two suitcases in the back. Most of your clothes. A lot of cash. It's old, but it's still American currency. People hoarded it in the early days until it wasn't really good for anything. Then they just had it lying around. I've been visiting some empty houses. I gathered up quite a bit of it, well over ten thousand dollars. I suppose that's still a lot.'

'Daddy…' Georgia said. Her voice had gone cold.

I kept saying what I'd planned to say. I knew if I stopped, even for a moment, I'd never finish.

'I made a list of some ideas to get you started. I don't know, it could be all wrong. After you get a room, go to the police station, tell them you don't have any identification, that you need some help. When they ask why there's no record of you, tell them you were raised religious. Off the grid. Your folks didn't trust the government. But they're dead now, so you had to go away. You're so creative, I know you'll think of something.'

Georgia tried to get out of the car, but I'd flipped the automatic locks. She didn't even know how to get the door open. I didn't want to think about all the other things she didn't know. She would learn.

'Don't tell anyone you've got the money. And whatever you do, don't tell them where you're from. If they find out they might… there's just no reason for them to know, that's all.'

She shouted, 'You're just going to leave me here?!'

I couldn't remember the last time she raised her voice to me.

'You can't stay in that dead town. You belong out in the world.'

Her face flushed and she started sucking in huge gulps of air. Her hands balled into fists atop her knees.

'It was Momma's gift to me! It's still upstairs on my bedside table!'

I squeezed the steering wheel so hard I thought it would snap off. That antique case, she never went anywhere without it. How could I have forgotten it?

"Momma gave it to me for Christmas!' Her voice dropped to nearly a whisper. 'She's gonna hate you for this.'

I told her I knew that was a possibility. I didn't tell her that I was sure if they'd had to say goodbye, we never would have left.

I reached across her to open the glove compartment for a pair of old brown work gloves. I slipped them on so nobody would see the teeth growing out of my fingertips. My shoes and shirt hid the rest. I couldn't have anybody spotting me and risk revealing where Georgia had come from.

I unlocked the Jeep and dragged the suitcases out of the trunk. I near had to drag Georgia out as well. She fought against me for a minute until she fell into my arms, crying. A couple of people standing out front of the motel were watching us, an older lady and a woman in a cleaner's uniform. They looked normal enough, as best I could remember. Maybe the world outside hadn't changed too much. Could be there was still room in it somewhere.

I held Georgia for a long time, the last time, told her that I loved her. She said something else to me, something just between us, but I can't think of it now, or maybe ever, not if I want to keep going. I still have Jenny to look after.

And then I drove off, back the way I came. I left her there, in the parking lot of that motel, alone, not sure what would become of her, but at least knowing she had a chance. It felt like some awful, aching thing inside me had finally been yanked free, and now there's only a raw, red hole in its place that would never be filled again.

CLAIRE OLESON

THE BIRTH
OF YOUR
DAUGHTER

Lauren straddled the rusted two-speed bike. She was letting fear work her open from the navel up. It was eight hilly miles to the nearest town – a breeze for any engine, but a punishment for a bike. She knew herself to be, mostly and simply, afraid and incapable. Her inner thigh strained as she pushed off the seat. The RV was behind her, unhitched from a driving force, needing things.

It was high summer, mid-nineties. She had cut her hair down to a two-inch thing and thrown the coppery refuse out the back window. Cicadas gnashed the air into a kind of metal. The black tank needed emptying, but she would have to drive the trailer to a sewer hookup, and they were, right then, camping illegally in a tuck of Indiana forest and far from any access.

Some two-ish years ago, Lauren had held Hemmy at a college party. They had been on an off-brown couch in someone's duplex escalating how much they could give to one another. How they could, with ease, just dive into living together.

The strangerhood of the other person did not bother either of them. The fact that Lauren did not go to college and was running herself into the ground with underpaid work did not scare Hemmy off.

Hemmy had a vodka-something in her hand. Her legs were tucked up underneath her. Lauren had her dead dad's coat on and a headache she'd broken apart on a few fingers of someone else's whiskey. One of them had said something like, 'So we actually wouldn't need a lot of money,' and the other had said back, 'Yeah, we wouldn't need money, not really,' and these sentences had seen them buy a second-hand trailer after Hemmy's graduation and start parking it in parts of woods. They usually did not pay or check if they should be paying. Hemmy liked having a townie with her. Lauren liked escaping the circle of working and hurting and only having, after weeks and weeks of minor abuse, like twenty dollars.

They worked well together. They were cheap. They ate well. They wore each other's clothes. Hemmy used to be smaller than her, but perhaps out of some survival awareness and a desire to conserve closet space, she had graciously put on twelve bright little pounds so their waists could trade pants with greater ease. Hemmy drank lightly, Lauren smoked on the weekends. They'd gotten so close through the shared food and clothes that Hemmy's sense of a body had swelled up to include the whole RV. She was two people in one column of metal. She was a four-handed, two-headed beast of rebellious survival with no pension, no home insurance, no husband. They'd been here in this one spot for a few good months. Enough time that Hemmy had bothered to plant some tomato seeds. Lauren watered them now, kicking back the rage in her head as she pressed a thumb over the hose nozzle and let the water blitz the new green shoots. Who knew if they'd actually get to fruiting.

Hemmy wrote book reviews and read unpublished novel after unpublished novel on her laptop screen. From Lauren's understanding, she edited things, and money dripped from an invisibly-positioned IV into their little bank account. She would tell Lauren about the landscape of contemporary fiction. About what was rotting and what was thrumming with viable commercial life. Lauren was straight from nowhere, strung-wide on a series of shitty little waitressing gigs in Indiana, and now, because of how they lived, free from doing that labour. Nothing made her want the restaurant jobs back: the asking, the hours, the heat, the steam, the oil burns, the men yelling from other rooms. The Southern-Northern feeling of rural Indiana. Her mostly low tips. She fixed the truck and maintained the RV. She led any social connections they tried to make in town. She offered vague mechanic services when they caught wind of broken things. But again, not much was needed. Wonder bread and gas station provisions and jerky and one dinner out a month, somewhere with more booths than tables, came easy. She was on Hemmy's data plan and they shared one phone. She had overwatered the tomatoes before she turned the hose off. The black tank needed emptying.

Lauren had shirked college, shirked her mother, shirked her father's long dying that came so slow and clear that it was practically a scheduled event from a decade out. She was happy: living with a girlfriend with no huge concerns, still hovering on her mother's health insurance, teaching herself everything from truck brake maintenance to postmodern literary lenses from the comfort of her off-grid living room/ dining room/ kitchen. She had been helping, recently, reading things along with Hemmy and giving notes, some of which Hemmy would actually write down and send on. Hemmy would touch the side of her face when she'd done well: little palm cupping her jaw, no assumption of dullness from Lauren's lack of higher education. Hemmy had given her, frankly, most of an English degree by talking. By being so patient. By sharing the PDFs of books that were coming out in two months and pirated classics alike. The black tank needed emptying.

There was a river not far from their campsite. Lauren would go there and try to wash the terrible feeling clear from her skin. A stagnant, sore kind of waiting. She had dragged huge river stones together near a bend to make a small pool a month ago. A present for Hemmy. The water still moved through, but it paused, gathered a circular breath, and held a cooler temperature in a patch of shade before it left. The walk there was twenty-five minutes long. Lauren cried the whole way, holding herself by a bubbling, collapsing middle. To start the walk, she had to move over the dark indents in the ground in front of the trailer. Those tire grooves. The last fucking thing Hemmy left before she went out, pre-dawn, with the truck. You really just had to drive to get to town. Biking there was a brutality they reserved for emergencies. Lauren could not tell if it was biking-time yet.

The river was sweet and cold. It unlatched the body from the body. Lauren slipped into it in old underwear, aware that she might now be a woman alone in semi-wilderness, rather than the butcher unit to a couple. She might be one-headed and two-handed. There were no houses visible from either riverbank. Not even the edge of some farm field, noticeable by a lessening of tree cover, fizzled on the horizon. It was a sizable "alone." Still, she didn't *not* worry about men when she undressed, when a rabbit moved, when the sunlight changed, or when a first-year buck tried his two-point antlers on a birch tree.

Lauren usually went by "Laur," and Helena went by "Hemmy." Only one of those shortenings made any sense, but it did not change that they were both there now, landed in a lifestyle, in a pattern of calling one another the same things, divorced from the lives any parent had hoped from them. The black tank needed emptying. Laur had to get through time faster, to figure out if she was ruined, to figure out if she had been abandoned in full. A girlfriend or a woman (two different things, to her). A camper or an unhoused person quietly excusing themselves from the title out of hope. A lifestyle or a way to end up dying because, some night, a raccoon would give her rabies or a stray piece of metal would get some corner of some finger, and she'd write it off, and then she'd wake up tetanus-full and doomed. She did not know if Hemmy was angry or dead or worse: back to being Helena somewhere. Laur moved in the water. A knife-cloud of minnows gestured with light. She went under and felt the cold shock spark her brain into just an animal, just for a moment. The black tank. The truck gone with Hemmy in it. Their PO box three counties away.

How many days should she give to Hemmy before Laur broke the world on her thoughts? How many hours were there before she was single, before every movement she made would go unseen, unreinforced, unsafe? How long before she should try to bike to some public library and log onto her shared bank account to see if it was gone, if the password was changed, if she was being killed by isolation? She didn't even know where one was. She wouldn't even be able to get the time if it weren't for her dad's wristwatch in the little dresser: a little antique bygone thing that *now* may or may not be absolutely critical to her survival. How long? Those batteries would die eventually. She probably wouldn't file any taxes. How far could she move the little trailer if she grabbed it by the hitch and pushed a life-or-death feeling into the centre of her chest and dug? Two inches? Anything longer than her hair? She was pretty strong from how she'd been living. She had been cutting wood and sometimes they would catch a rabbit and she would undo the rabbit from the rabbit and make it into something to keep her girl warm and going. The fucking black tank. She might have to start shitting in the woods now. She might have to get lower to the ground. If she opened her eyes underwater, she could make out the fuzzed shots of light. The passing accumulations of blurred bugs, of lost worms, of algae conspiring into green moving fists. Laur came up for air.

She remembered a river out of her childhood, a place they'd go when her dad was still upright and dangerous. These were canoe trips with one of her dad's visiting friends, a man insistent on teaching her how to catch and preserve the river bugs.

They'd nab them in small nets and then drop the little bodies into clear vials filled with alcohol where they'd die, but stay whole, stay legible, stay preserved, as an education on bodies. On the ways life could be. She stopped thinking about Hemmy and started trying to remember the Latin names for everything smaller than her fingers. The river in front of her lit up.

The nymphs were the easiest thing to find this time of year, their translucent edges flexing, their adulthoods suspended. She could remember her dad proffering a hydropsyche he looped in a thin net, years back. Its wings were tucked; his nailbeds were shadowed with silt; there were two six-packs in the canoes. She learned how to hold the bugs in her hands with a pressure that fell perfectly between pinning and crushing. She had been eleven, waiting to see if her dad or his friend would be the one to start drinking first. She'd been dutiful and attentive. She'd leaned in when either of them raised up the next crumb-sized thing they'd caught and began explaining it into a little life.

She kept the vials for a few years. Thin, as shakable as snowglobes, though she knew not to shake them. She was respectful of the thumb-narrow insect deaths. She would, sometimes, tip the drowned graves very slowly to watch them fall or ascend. An adolescent water boatman would sail, eyes first, towards the cork. All snow. Oh, what about winter? Winter alone without the car. The black tank. She got out of the river and grabbed her clothes in a wet hand and walked herself, like you'd walk a stranger's dog, back to the RV. What about Hemmy's hands and her clothes? Her side table mirror and a few of her real books. Those were there. But her laptop, her wallet, her passport, and her backpack were gone. Laur took in the stock of items in the trailer like they were all things balancing a see-saw: how much taken away meant someone was out of love with you? How much left behind meant that they must, if you cleaned the rooms, come back down to you? Laur brushed her teeth for four uninterrupted minutes and spit out the window where her old hair still burned a glossy auburn when a dash of sun passed over it. She knew where the wristwatch was but didn't want to get it out. Didn't want to put numbers on the day. She'd sit outside, she decided, and watch the light fall and wait to see if she was still a girlfriend today. She kept touching her hair: new. She kept checking the tomatoes, the gas tank, the farmer's almanack she'd bought. None of them moved or told her anything good. None of them gave her something easy to fight. She sat on the bike again and thought about the distance before dismounting. Her inner thigh rang: that light strain returning. She'd make a fire.

During her college years, Hemmy had sent Laur party invite after party invite until Laur's social life was far closer to that of a middle-class person with a college fund than of someone bending over counters for breakfast orders. Of any unindebted-rich young person. Of anyone who thought of the future without a genuine dread for the mere feeling of time moving. With her back braced against clapboard apartment walls, Laur (with great relief) let Hemmy kiss her up into a new social class. The lights and sound thrummed against her shoulders like a set of cell-paned insect wings. They would not need a lot of money. Hemmy had still had a tongue piercing back then: the metal ball the size of a water penny beetle in either of their mouths. The black tank.

Laur hauled out the old burnt logs from the fire circle in front of the RV. If she was alone now, she thought, there would be no way she'd be able to move to a sewer hookup to empty the black tank before the place went rancid. She stopped before putting fresh wood in. She might as well treat the day like she was alone. She took her ash-gilded hands to her face and pressed. She might treat the day like it was a decade. Like she would need to become a person going after money again. Like she had been left for dead, just the way she'd come in. She wiped snot from crying up her face. The coming evening was warm enough already: a fire would be a redundant, comfortless heat.

She got the shovel out of their utility closet and started digging a moat behind the trailer that led downhill. This was something to do for an hour while the dark speckled in. She watched the bodies of worms become exposed like wet, thrashing gems. She dug through them. She wiped her fear-swollen face and half-hoped the whole thing might just come loose. She thought about her mother, who was alone, but in a house and not the woods.

Hemmy had been good to Laur every night but one, over eight months ago, when she'd made a mistake and slept with a man and of course the condom found a way to become a mouth instead of a wall and of course Hemmy swelled up with a new finger-sized life and of course her apologies were some of the most well-written, true bits of language Laur had ever taken in. There was no question Laur would take her back. The man had been a pharmacist too, offered her every available version of a medical off-ramp. Hemmy had, after asking Laur, elected to see the thing through despite this. What was Laur meant to say: no? Suspend the potential for potential life? Keep it as a dangling, vialed concept and not a person? This would have been too much to expect. But she had expected it, nonetheless. She was on Hemmy's phone bill. She was in Hemmy's love and twin bed and hope and ideations. She was often thumb-deep in Hemmy's middle. Laur went to the black tank and attached the hose. She pointed the mouth downhill into her ditch, the skeleton to a river, and unlatched the access.

Flowing wild, the waste stunk; the thick smell of it got into her mouth and nose and chest. She could feel it moving in the wet air. She could feel how it should revolt her. But it didn't, not now, as the terrible little thought came to her: what if the shit and the tomatoes were the last things they'd made happen together? They were, Laur decided, they were, and she had already ruined one of them with overwatering. Hemmy had gone off with him. Her body had drawn her back, though she had not meant it to, and they were devoted because of what had happened between them. It would be better for the baby. There were no notes anywhere, in the RV or outside of it, to say that Laur was still loved and needed and included in the life they'd been having. Hemmy had gone at nine months and wouldn't be coming back to move the RV, to change the lights, to sit in the river on sky-gold evenings like it was a marriage.

Normally, Laur would wear a mask for the black tank and the sewage would go into sewage, not the air, not the visible landscape. But what was there left to keep clean and safe? She still wanted Hemmy in her mouth and chest. When this all stopped, she'd flush out the greywater tank and then the freshwater one. This process was meant to be self-cleaning. The sewage washed from the hose by other, cleaner wastes. The space would still reek. Would attract insects she didn't know the names of. Would show her how bad things could get, how fast.

She was still holding the hose, spilling darkly down the hill, when the dim, post-dinner world was cut with the salt of headlights. She whipped around, shit spilling from the pipe's mouth. Out came her. Out came Hemmy holding something close to her chest and out, from the other door, came her pharmacist with his hair longer than Laur's, in his mid-thirties, so gentle as he closed the truck door and looped around to help Hemmy.

'I am so sorry. Jesus. It all happened so fast and you sleep so well,' Hemmy offered, her face raked clean of fear and energy alike. It looked like snow. Like some winter Laur had planned to take alone. She still couldn't tell if they were together and she was apart. Hemmy covered her nose and mouth.

'God, did the black tank burst?'

'No,' Laur started, unsure of how to begin, refuse still coursing below her fist. 'No, it's just... I couldn't move the RV without the truck. It needed emptying. I sort of. Well, I believed you'd kinda gone *gone*.' Laur looked at Hemmy and her pharmacist, whose face was placid and open, only slightly recoiling at the horrible smell, the horrible sight, the terrible thing he'd brought Hemmy back to see.

'Are you gone?' Laur asked the woman and her baby and her baby's father while they all stood in front of her.

'She's back,' Peter said, aware now that Laur did not believe in a good, reliable world that brought loved things back to their lovers. 'You two, you should maybe get two phones.' He was smiling, clasping his face, tears welling from the rancid air. 'And it went well, really, she did so good, your girl.' Peter pointed at Hemmy and her bundle, which reached a worm-coloured arm into the light.

'I'll be around if you want, and not if you don't. My own car's back at the main road. I thought you might see it parked and get an… an understanding.' Peter took off his glasses and turned to start hacking against a birch tree.

'Oh Laur, goddamn I'm so sorry, you must've been scared, were you scared?' Even now, Hemmy's face went up in sympathy. Where was her exhaustion, her hobble, her anger at Lauren missing something so huge because what? She could not be woken or thrown fast enough from her medication-thick sleep?

'She's early. She must… she must be so small.'

'She's small but she's good. She's all good.' Hemmy was smiling, looking down at a face half hers, half something else's that Laur could not see. Laur set down the hose that still gurgled with things half hers, half Hemmy's. How long ago had her love been at the hospital, waiting for the worst pain in her life to come cleaving, white and calcifying, through her centre? Waiting for that baby the three of them had not decided how to know yet. How hard had it been to know which direction to take it and name it and hold it? And for how long? And how had the labour been? And had *he* cried and held the baby, or had he gone down some hallway to look at a vending machine and read the names of sodas while she screamed? Which scene did Laur want to be true? How dedicated or how terrible should the man be? He was on one knee, posed in adoration to a wall of bark, his back to them, spitting into the dirt. He had not known, on the night, that Hemmy wasn't single. How much could Laur be allowed to hate him? How tired had he gotten?

'I want to see her, I think,' Laur said, knowing it was not enough to be saying. Knowing she'd ruined their campsite and they'd have to head out tonight and abandon their tomato project to keep the baby safe from the most dangerous of human substances now set loose across their mock-yard. How much pain had there been? Had she taken an epidural? Had the nurses warmed their manifold teal hands before they touched her for hours, before going over her like a river of expertise and attention and routine? Had they looked like married people while they waited?

Peter had turned back around. He was opening a duffle bag from which he would offer them the postnatal vitamin set and baby food and diapers, all free of charge. Laur did not know the baby's name, how warm the baby was, if the baby was ugly, if the baby would stay with them or not, if the baby would like her, if Peter hated them, what shape the hospital bill would take, what shape of stain Hemmy's broken water had made on the passenger seat of the truck as they'd set out in the dark to keep her loved one safe and good and whole and new.

'When you hold her,' Peter said, his arms in the space in front of him, 'hold her like this, with the head up, yeah?'

'Like this?' Laur responded, willing to take such stupid, obvious instruction as mimicking the posture, of raising the baby's imagined head above its imagined body slightly, of leaning in like she was being offered a new type of animal. She was. She held the posture. She smelled like something so much worse than dying.

'Yes,' Hemmy told her, smiling, her own baby in her arms 'Perfect, like that.'

Peter did not move to tell Hemmy that she didn't quite have it right; that the head was still too low in her hands; that the blood would pool a bit. He did not move, either, to applaud the perfect and frozen posture of Lauren, who was streaked with tube-digested shit and dotted with charcoal, snot-smeared and still wet, at the head and joints, with river water. The one who could hold the baby couldn't hold the baby. The other one who couldn't hold the baby could hold the baby.

Without being asked to, Laur rocked the air in front of her chest and waited to feel right. For a baby that she wasn't holding, a baby that wasn't crying, to somehow come to stop crying in her arms and know her.

THE AUTHORS

ELLIE ALLAN is a writer based in York (UK), recently finishing her LLM degree in Art Law at the University of York, having completed her undergraduate degree in Art History at NYU Abu Dhabi. She tends to write semi-autobiographical poetry and short stories in between researching graverobbers and intellectual property law.

ELLA BARRON CARTON is a short story writer and poet whose work focuses on relationships and nature, both natural and cultivated. Her work has appeared in *Abridged, Poetry Ireland Review*, and *New Word Order*. She lives in Cork City.

FINOLA CAHILL is a writer from Co. Mayo. Her poetry has appeared in *The London Magazine, Propel* and others. She won the 2023 Waterford Poetry Prize and the 2024 Listowel Writers Week Single Poem Award, and has been shortlisted for multiple other prizes, including the Máirtín Crawford Short Story Award.

LYNDSEY CROAL is a Scottish author of strange and speculative fiction, with work published in over eighty magazines and anthologies, including *Apex*, *Analog SF*, and *Weird Tales*. She's a Scottish Book Trust New Writers Awardee, British Fantasy Award Finalist, and former Hawthornden Fellow. Her longer works include *Have You Decided on Your Question* (Shortwave), *Limelight and Other Stories* (Shortwave), *The Girl With Barnacles for Eyes* (*Split Scream Volume Five*, Tenebrous Press), and, forthcoming, *Dark Crescent* (Luna Press). **www.lyndseycroal.co.uk**

STEVE DENEHAN lives in Kildare, Ireland with his wife Eimear and daughter Robin. He is the author of two chapbooks and five poetry collections. Winner of the Anthony Cronin Poetry Award and twice winner of *Irish Times'* New Irish Writing, his numerous publication credits include *Poetry Ireland Review* and *Westerly*.

SOFIE DE SMYTER is an English TA and student counsellor at KU Leuven (Belgium). Words in *Profiles*, *The Belfield Literary Review*, *Aesthetica Creative Writing Award 2024*, *Litro*, *Exposition Review* and *Frustrated Writers' Anthology #2*.

MARISOL KARCS is an MFA candidate at Iowa State University. She likes to write about odd things happening, about jobs that suck, and about queerness. She also likes snails.

GRACE KULLY *(she/her/hers)* is a Creative Writing MA student at Queen's University, Belfast from New Jersey, USA. She graduated from Villanova University in 2023, where she studied English Literature and Disability Studies. Her published work is forthcoming in *Kaleidoscope Magazine*. She loves rainy days inside with a book.

SHANE LARKIN is a writer and editor from Meath. He is the winner of the 2023 New Flash Fiction Prize. His work has appeared in *Splonk*, *Best Small Fictions*, and others. He is a contributing editor for the *New Flash Fiction Review*.

SEAN MICHAEL is an aspiring writer who lives in the South Denver Metro area. When he isn't writing horror, thrillers, and other speculative fiction, Sean can be found reading, hiking, skiing, kayaking, and enjoying life with his wife, family, and friends.

BRYAN MILLER is a Minneapolis-based writer and performer. His work has appeared in more than a dozen journals and anthologies including *The Bombay Literary Magazine*, *The Drabblecast*, *CBS Late Late Show with Craig Ferguson*, and *Sirius/XM* radio.

CLAIRE OLESON is a queer writer and 2020 Fiction Fellow at the Center for Fiction. She is an Assistant Editor at the *Kenyon Review*. Her work has been published by *Joyland*, the *LA Review of Books*, and *Brink*, among others. Her chapbook of short stories debuted May, 2020 from Newfound Press.

C.T. O'MAHONY is a Kilkenny-based writer with a love of all things science fiction, fantasy and horror. She won a place on the Irish Writers Centre National Mentoring Programme 2022, and won an Artlinks Emerging Artist Award in 2023. She's currently working on her first novel.

BRIÁ PURDY is an artist and writer based in Paris, France. She is the editor of *The Head of a Woman*, a surrealist print zine.

DORIAN ROSE primarily writes queer speculative fiction. He occasionally tries to branch out, but aliens keep happening. He's currently working on a fantasy novel while completing an MSc in Creative Writing at the University of Edinburgh. He also holds an MA in Queer Studies, and a BA(Hons) in Philosophy.

Sans.
PRESS